TOUCH THE SKY

TOUCH THE SKY

Aviation and Other Stories

David Helms

iUniverse, Inc.
New York Lincoln Shanghai

Touch the Sky
Aviation and Other Stories

Copyright © 2005 by David Helms

iUniverse books may be ordered through booksellers or by contacting:

iUniverse
2021 Pine Lake Road, Suite 100
Lincoln, NE 68512
www.iuniverse.com
1-800-Authors (1-800-288-4677)

ISBN-13: 978-0-595-37019-1 (pbk)
ISBN-13: 978-0-595-81427-5 (ebk)
ISBN-10: 0-595-37019-5 (pbk)
ISBN-10: 0-595-81427-1 (ebk)

Printed in the United States of America

For Andrea

CONTENTS

▼

THE SKY QUEEN

Where thou thyself dost air, the queen 'o the sky

—William Shakespeare

DEPARTURE

Two men dressed in brown flight suits stood on the ramp near the nose of the ship, their eyes roaming thoughtfully over her graceful lines.

"Okay, Pop, got the check list?"

"Right here, sir."

"Right, let's see if she's ready to fly."

Second Lieutenant Pierre "Dan'l" Boun, the co-pilot, and Master Sergeant George "Pop" Loudon, the flight engineer, began the ritual of the pre-flight inspection. There was an easy familiarity between the two that was typical of flight crews. This ease resulted from a bond forged by mutual respect and interdependence so necessary to flight operations. Each member of this five-man crew was a highly trained specialist.

They made an unlikely pair. Dan'l was a commissioned officer from Baton Rouge, Louisiana. A graduate of the Air Cadet Program, he had earned his wings less than a year ago. He was a short, stocky, dark skinned, twenty-two year old. When he spoke, it was with a musical lilt that revealed his Cajun heritage. His eyes twinkled continuously, and he was always laughing and joking about something. His last name Boun, when pronounced in the French way, sounded vaguely like "Boone." So everyone just called him Dan'l.

Pop Loudon was almost his direct opposite. Pop was a non-commissioned officer with fifteen years service from the small hill country town of Three Rivers, California. He was tall, lanky, and fair with a shock of straw-colored hair that protruded defiantly from under his grease-stained flight cap. His speech was laconic and had a pronounced western drawl. At thirty-three, he was the oldest member of the crew. He was also the only one with children, although his wife had divorced him some six years ago. So, naturally, he carried the nickname "Pop." He and Dan'l were the oldest and youngest members of Captain Richard "Dusty" Rhodes' crew.

"How long you been in the air force, Pop? You fly with Orville and Wilbur?" asked Dan'l mischievously, his eyes following his flashlight beam over the nose wheel steering mechanism.

"Joined up in '29. Reckon you was just a squirt."

"Well mind you don't trip over your beard, Dad," remarked Dan'l with a giggle.

"Never mind about the beard, Sonny. At least I'm old enough to grow one." Pop was a hard man to needle.

As they progressed outward under the leading edge of the left wing to the engines, their mood turned professionally serious.

"You gave these engines a careful look, right Sergeant?"

"Uh huh. Had some help from the ground crew."

"You run 'em up?"

"Yes sir. They're singing like meadowlarks on a mountain mornin'."

"Number two was surging a bit the last couple of hours yesterday."

"Yeah, I saw your comment on the Form One," replied Pop, tugging at his ear. "I gave that engine a complete inspection, including bench-testing all thirty-six spark plugs. That engine is fine."

"Good. You know how the old man is. The first thing he looks at is the Form One," said Dan'l casting a furtive glance toward the flight operations shack.

"Everything's signed off. The *Sky Queen's* fine. It took most of the day," Pop complained.

"Well, Sergeant, what else were you going to do on a beautiful April day in lovely Labrador?" Dan'l retorted, teasingly.

"Sleep!"

"Oh that," replied Dan'l, chuckling.

Sky Queen was a USAAF C-54 Skymaster, #42-41734. At some previous time, somewhere, someone had painted a picture on her nose. It was a sexy rendering of Glenda, the beautiful good witch from the movie *The Wizard of Oz,* complete with gold crown and magic wand. Instead of a full-skirted ball gown, however, Glenda was wearing only a pair of lacy panties. She wore a knapsack on her back with the straps strategically placed to cover the nipples of her full and shapely breasts. Her lovely face with a come hither smile looked downward toward the ramp. No matter where you stood, she seemed to be looking directly at you. The effect was startlingly suggestive. Other than the artist's rendering, there was no name or slogan to accompany it. For a while, the crew called her *Glenda.* Later, they just started affectionately calling her *Sky Queen*. No one could remember why or when it started.

With an overall length of almost 94 feet, a wingspan of over 117 feet, and a height of almost 28 feet, *Sky Queen* was the largest cargo airplane in the army inventory. She was even larger than the B-17 and B-24 bombers of her day. Weighing in at an empty weight of 38,000 pounds, she could easily carry an additional 24,000 pounds of cargo, passengers, crew, and fuel. Frequently, though, she exceeded that limitation because of the urgencies of war.

Her four Pratt & Whitney Twin Wasp, eighteen-cylinder, radial engines each connected to a large, three-blade, Hamilton–Standard full-feathering propeller developed a total of almost 6,000 horsepower. They pulled the *Sky Queen* and her payload through the sky at a respectable cruising speed of 208 knots. She had an operating ceiling of 10,000 feet. She could go higher, but her cabin and flight deck were not pressurized. She typically cruised in the 4,000 to 9,000 foot range for crew and passenger comfort. The C-54s were solid and dependable, well loved by the men who flew them. In nearly 80,000 crossings of the North Atlantic, there were only three losses.

The air in the flight operations shack at Goose Bay, Labrador, was stuffy and warm. The small room was filled with departing and arriving aircrews. The few men on one side of the counter had a weary and harried look. They represented weather, navigation, flight planning, weight and balance, air/sea rescue, fueling and similar disciplines. Goose Bay was not the principal departure or arrival field for Air Transport Command's North Atlantic routes. Stephenville, Newfoundland, usually fulfilled that purpose. Yesterday, however, a rogue weather system had completely closed that facility. All traffic had been re-routed to Goose Bay. It was like New York City's Penn Station on any Friday afternoon.

Dusty Rhodes was a fine pilot and a good aircraft commander, although somewhat vain. He had dark good looks, an athletic physique, a thin pencil mustache, and a liking for tailored uniforms. Even his flight suits were tailored. He resembled Clark Gable. His crew at one time had started calling him "Rhett," the Clark Gable character in *Gone with the Wind*. But Dusty quickly discouraged that, and the crew dropped it.

His hometown was Asheville, North Carolina, and he sometimes would tell people that his family was one of those mentioned in the Thomas Wolfe novel, *Look Homeward, Angel*. Of course, a lot of people from Asheville said the same thing, but in Dusty's case it was probably true. His family had wealth and his parents had been active in the Asheville social scene. Tragically, they were both killed just prior to the outbreak of the war. One Saturday night, while driving to the prestigious Grove Park Inn for the annual Mayor's Ball, their car was hit head-on by a drunk driver. Ironically, the drunk driver sustained only minor injuries.

Dusty's fingers drummed on the counter. He was a patient man, but patience had its limits. "Hey!" he called to the man directly across the counter from him, "Have you got my weather package and fuel loading yet?"

"Coming right up, sir."

"Yeah, you said that ten minutes ago."

"Here it is, Captain. It just came in."

The young lieutenant's tie was pulled askew, and he had dark stains under his arms. His long blonde hair was down in his face. His thick horn-rimmed glasses had slipped to the end of his nose and appeared in imminent danger of falling off. He looked somewhat like a cartoon character from the comic strip, "Terry and the Pirates."

"I had your weather, but the ramp guys are running behind on fueling. We're not used to having so many aircraft here at one time," he said apologetically.

"Well, let's have it. The war isn't going to wait for you and me, now is it?"

"No sir. Sorry, Captain," he replied as he handed the documents across the counter.

Now that Captain Rhodes had what he wanted, he could afford to be charitable.

"No sweat, son. It all counts toward twenty."

Dusty was making reference to the oft-quoted phrase referring to a twenty-year career in the military. He had been commissioned in 1940 and was considering doing just that after the war. He carried his package to a nearby table where the remaining two members of *Queen's* crew were seated, poring over their own paper work.

First Lieutenant John "Smilin' Jack" Carter was a serious minded introvert from Coeur D' Alene, Idaho. Like Pop Loudon, he also was tall and lanky, as most westerners seemed to be. His hair had been light brown at one time, but was now thinning. He had a nervous habit of frequently running a hand over his head, especially when he was engrossed in a navigation problem. You got the impression that he had just worn it all away. His nickname "Smilin' Jack" referred perversely to the fact that he seldom if ever smiled. He was a damn good flight navigator, though—one of the best. His idea of having fun on a Saturday night was to study star charts and run through tricky navigation problems and trigonometric functions. Some of the other crew members were fond of commenting—behind his back—that he would get married when he found a woman who could use a navigator's octant and shoot better star fixes than he.

Staff Sergeant Francis "Tex" Williams, like every other person named "Tex" was a native of Texas. In his case, he called San Angelo home. Actually, he didn't know where he was from, or even if he was from Texas at all. He was the unwanted result of a quick and sweaty union between a drunken cowboy and an equally drunk dance hall girl one hot summer night—somewhere. He was raised in an orphanage in San Angelo, so he called that home.

As radio operators went, Tex was probably about average. He saw to it that his equipment was always in good working condition, but was usually behind in keeping his radio manuals updated. Changes were constantly being published, and it was his job to file the new pages and discard the out-of-date ones. His speed with Morse telegraphy was somewhat slower than average, but he was accurate. He had one skill that was unique, though. He could listen to the squeals, pops, sizzles, and shrieks that frequently came over the radio circuit and hear the dits and dahs of Morse code where others could hear nothing but noise. Tex always said that it resulted from a habit acquired at the orphanage. He learned to tune out the bedlam of the other kids when he wanted to escape for a little while. On balance, Dusty was glad to have him.

"How ya doin', Tex"

"Fine, Captain," Tex replied, grinning boyishly.

"Got all the dope you need?"

"Yes sir. None of the low power radio beacons shown as out-of service in the latest bulletins should affect us. Dernycross Radio is down, but we can work around that."

"All your radios up and running?"

"Yes sir, they are," Tex answered. He was proud of the fact that his equipment was always in working order.

"Good man," said Dusty, placing his hand lightly on Tex's shoulder. He didn't speak to his navigator. He knew from experience that it was better to leave Jack alone until his navigation chores were finished.

Dusty sat down, pulled a crumpled pack of Chesterfields out of the pocket on the left sleeve of his flight suit, and produced a silver Ronson lighter from a similar pocket on the right sleeve. His wife, Joy, had given him the lighter upon his promotion to captain. It had his initials engraved in gothic letters on one side and a miniature set of captain's bars on the other side. It was a cherished possession. Lighting his cigarette, he stowed the pack and the lighter back where they belonged.

Taking a long puff, he proceeded to study the weather and meteorological data affecting his route of flight and destination. The data confirmed his hunch about the weather. The system that closed Stephenville yesterday had moved eastward into the Atlantic, dutifully following the prevailing westerly winds. However, there appeared to be an area of acceptable weather over the North Atlantic extending eastward from St. Johns, Newfoundland, to a point about a thousand miles west of Ireland. But the weather from there onward was forecast to be marginal to bad, especially over the British Isles. "Well, what else is new," grumbled Dusty as he studied the dizzying swirl of isobars on the chart in front of him. Experience had taught him that weather over Scotland and Northern England was bad most of the time, no matter what the season. Furthermore, it was usually worse than forecast.

A tap on his shoulder broke his concentration. It was Smilin' Jack. "The flight plan is finished, Captain."

"Will our planned fuel load be okay?"

"Yeah, if the forecast winds are anywhere near right. I threw in a little gas for Mama."

"Gas for Mama" was a euphemism. It referred to the time-honored habit of flight crews everywhere to carry some extra fuel that would not appear on any manifest or weight and balance form. More than once, it had been the difference between life and death, especially over water and inhospitable terrain.

Dusty smiled knowingly. "Okay. Anything else?"

"This just came in," responded Jack, handing over a Teletype message.

Unfolding the paper, Dusty read the terse message:

DATE: 1433Z17APR44
FROM: CMDR, 40TH ATW, USAAF WRI
TO: CMDR RCAF YQX
FOR: R.O. Rhodes, CPT, USAAF (USAAF C-54 42-41734)

OPERATION IMMEDIATE

ADV THS HQ FMP ETA BLB.

FTC:
JONATHAN W. WILLIAMSTON, MAJ, ADJ

Translating the message, Dusty read, "Advise this headquarters by the fastest means possible your estimated time of arrival at RAF Blackbush."

"Operation Immediate, huh?" Dusty squinted at Jack and said; "I think the old man's got his drawers in a twist again."

"Looks like it."

"Well, Jack, what is our ETA?"

"It's twenty-one hundred nautical miles to Blackbush via Prestwick. With the forecast winds, our flight time should be ten hours and eighteen minutes."

"Another damn rump-buster," growled Dusty. "Okay, file it. Assume wheels up in forty-five minutes."

"Hell, Dusty, with all this traffic on the ground we'll be lucky to be airborne two hours from now."

"No." Dusty smiled waving the message and stowing it in a pocket of his flight suit. "Temporarily I've got a little pull around here. I'll take care of the message. You file that flight plan, notify the crew, and have Sergeant Loudon round up our passengers. I'm off to see the Wizard. Hubba Hubba; let's get this show on the road."

En Route

Dan'l called out the pre-takeoff checklist items as Dusty verified each one:
"Engine checks."
"Complete"
"Hydraulic pressures."
"Okay."
"Flaps and trim."
"Set for takeoff."
"Parking brake."
"Off."
"Cabin doors and windows."
"Closed."
"Pre-takeoff checklist complete, Captain."
"Goosey tower, Army 1734 ready to go on Runway 31. Over."
"Army 1734, Goosey Tower. Wind is 280 at 15, altimeter 29.98. Contact Maritime Departure on 4220 when airborne. Cleared for takeoff Runway 31. So long."
"Army 1734 rolling. See ya."
Dusty's right hand pushed the four tall throttles on the quadrant between the two pilot seats while simultaneously pushing on the right rudder pedal to compensate for the left turning tendency. *Sky Queen's* four engines roared responsively.
Dan'l called off the airspeeds, "60…70…80…90…rotate."
Dusty eased back on the control wheel, and *Sky Queen* smoothly lifted her bulk from the runway.
"Gear up," Dusty called while pointing his right thumb at the cabin roof.
Dan'l gripped the large wheel-shaped knob near the throttle quadrant, pulled it toward him to clear the detent, and moved it upward firmly. This was followed immediately by the whine of hydraulics and the rumble of mechanical linkages as the three sets of wheels unlocked and folded into the belly of the plane.
"Cruise climb, Captain. 160."

"Engineer, set climb power. Flaps up, Dan'l," responded Dusty.

"Climb power set," The flight engineer's station had its own set of engine controls and gauges. Pop adjusted his four black throttles and four blue propeller control knobs to the required settings.

"Flaps coming up."

Queen's crew was functioning smoothly.

Everyone started to relax after the tension of takeoff had passed. The *Sky Queen* settled into her 160-knot cruise climb configuration.

"Once more skill and daring have overcome abject terror. We cheated death again," said Dan'l humorously, a large grin splitting his face.

"What do you mean? We ain't there yet," growled Pop continuing their Abbot and Costello act.

"Navigator to A/C, recommend initial course 058."

"058 it is." Dusty turned the control wheel to the right and monitored the heading gyro as *Sky Queen* banked to the northeast.

For the next thirteen minutes, they climbed into the dim northern sky toward their assigned cruising altitude of 7,000 feet. They passed through one cloud layer at 2,500 and a second one at 4,800. A thin layer was forming at about 25,000, but at the moment *Sky Queen* was in the clear.

Presently, Dan'l called out, "Passing 7,000 Captain."

"Roger." Dusty deliberately allowed *Sky Queen* to level off momentarily at 7,100. The indicated airspeed increased to 175 knots, at which time he pushed the control wheel forward to ease *Sky Queen* back to her assigned altitude and set the trim wheels for a configuration that would provide the least drag.

"Engineer, give me cruise power—65%."

"Stand by, Captain," replied Pop as he consulted his power charts for the correct settings. "Twenty-two inches and 2050 RPM. Fuel is 55."

"Okay, set it. I'll handle the mixture."

"Twenty-two and 2050. Wilco!"

"Cowl flaps closed," Dusty called after waiting a few minutes for the cylinder head temperatures to cool down and stabilize.

"Cowl flaps coming closed. Engine temps still okay," Pop said.

"Okay Dan'l, set the auto-pilot."

Boun turned the black knob labeled A/P from "Off" to "On." They both felt the reassuring control kick as the autopilot took over flying the airplane.

Dusty adjusted the fuel flow with the four red mixture control levers until the corresponding fuel flow meters read 55 gallons per hour.

"Navigator, burning 55 per engine."

"Roger. Thank you," Smilin' Jack responded crisply, entering the readings into his navigation log. At his engineer's station, Pop was doing the same thing. Fuel was precious, and its total consumption and consumption rates were monitored and recorded religiously.

Lieutenant Carter and Sergeant Williams occupied spaces almost directly across the center aisle from each other behind the flight deck. Smilin' Jack's cubicle appeared neat and orderly, reflecting the man himself. The space Tex occupied was filled from floor to ceiling with radio equipment set in metal racks. The equipment constantly hummed and emitted heat. This, oddly enough, gave the place a rather contented and homey feel.

"Lieutenant, what do you know about sunspots?"

Jack raised his eyes from his work and looked curiously at his radioman a few feet away.

"Why do you ask?"

"I dunno," Tex replied, scratching the back of his neck thoughtfully, "I read somewhere that they can cause trouble with radio waves."

"Are you having trouble now?"

"Maybe."

"Well which is it, Sergeant? You're either having trouble or you're not."

"Well, sir, the circuits are much noisier than usual, and some of the normally reliable stations seem to have stopped transmitting. Anyhow, I'm not receiving them."

"All of them?"

"No, just a few so far."

Jack knew that sunspots were magnetic and originated from cool spots near the sun's surface. They bombarded the earth with hydrogen ions, sometimes called a solar wind. They appeared on an 11-year cycle. He had read recently where the earth was entering such a cycle. Solar winds did disrupt radio communications occasionally, sometimes severely. "I'd better start taking star fixes as soon as I can. Radio navigation might become a problem before this flight is over," Jack thought,

"You'd better notify Captain Rhodes, and let me know if it gets worse."

"Wilco, sir."

Just as Jack was reaching for his octant, he heard a voice over his shoulder.

"Do you mind if I step up to the flight deck?"

Jack picked up the instrument, swiveled in his chair, and turned to face the voice.

It was Colonel Kittering, one of their passengers.

"Not at all, sir. I'll tell the captain that you're coming."

Pressing his intercom switch Jack said, "A/C, Navigator."

"What's up, Jack?"

"Colonel Kittering would like a word with you, Dusty." .

"Okay, send him up."

"Captain Rhodes says he'll be pleased to see you, Colonel."

Travis W. Kittering IV was a tall, handsome man with an aristocratic air about him that seemed to match his name. He wore an impressive array of ribbons on his breast topped by the coveted silver and blue Combat Infantry Badge, indicating that he had actually been in combat. He did not wear the silver wings of a pilot or any other aircrew member.

"Now I wonder what he wants," mused Dusty. Their first meeting had been in January at a Pentagon function in Washington. Dusty's wing commander, Colonel Roger Smith, had introduced them. The conversation was cordial but short and focused mostly on Dusty's flying career. Dusty had the distinct impression that he was being sized up for some reason. Since nothing came of it in the next several months, he had nearly forgotten the incident. Then, two days ago, Colonel Smith had summoned Dusty to his office at McGuire Army Air Base at Wrightstown, New Jersey.

"I've got a special assignment for you, Captain Rhodes," Colonel Smith said in a more formal tone than he usually used with his aircraft commanders.

"You mean after this next trip to Burtonwood," Dusty said with a puzzled look.

"No, I mean right now," replied Smith reaching into his desk drawer and pulling out a folder. Dusty noticed the broad red diagonal stripe on the front with the words "Top Secret" stamped in red above it.

"Here are your orders and flight plan, but they are quite simple. You are to take four passengers and 15 bags of courier material from here to Blackbush. You know that airfield, don't you? It's just outside London."

"Yes sir, I do. But my aircraft is scheduled to take a critical load of medical supplies to the Burtonwood Air Depot. It's all classified Priority 1A. Probably has something to do with the invasion of Europe. The rumor mill says that's going to happen pretty soon. The aircraft is being loaded right now."

"Correction, Captain. Your aircraft is being offloaded right now. Your passengers and cargo should arrive within the next two hours. You will get them and their material aboard and depart on schedule."

"I imagine this has something to do with 'Operation Overlord'. General Eisenhower's headquarters is in London, you know," Smith said pointedly.

"Yes sir."

"Well, do you recall the Pentagon Colonel you met in Washington a while back?"

"Yes sir, I do." It was all starting to fall into place now.

"He's one of your passengers. In fact, he's in charge of the entire detail. Now it is quite unusual for full Colonels on Pentagon Staff to act as couriers. You understand?"

Dusty nodded, his mind now racing.

"That's all," said Smith dismissively.

Dusty saluted, did a crisp military about face, and stepped to the door. Just as his hand touched the doorknob, Colonel Smith's voce stopped him.

"Have a nice trip, Captain." And in a kinder less formal tone Smith added, "Good luck, Dusty."

"Thank you sir," Captain Rhodes replied, closing the door behind him, all the while wondering what the hell that last comment was all about.

Dusty was brought sharply back to the present by his co-pilot's cheery voice.

"Good evening, Colonel. Welcome to the bar at the Top of the Mark. Cocktails will be served shortly."

Frowning, Dusty glared at Dan'l. "Why don't you get yourself a cup of *coffee*, Lieutenant?"

Dan'l was smart enough to know when he was being dismissed.

"Thanks. I believe I will," he replied still grinning. He squirmed out of his seat and left the flight deck to the other two.

"Have a seat, Colonel."

"How is the ride back there," Dusty asked conversationally, knowing full well that there was something else on Kittering's mind.

"Fine, but my schedule is not."

"Uh huh," Dusty responded encouragingly.

"Look, Captain, I know you have no control over the weather, and that mechanical problems do crop up from time to time. But that's all behind us now. I understand that you normally use 65% power in cruise flight. Is that correct?"

"Yes sir." Here it comes, thought Dusty.

"Well it seems to me that if you used 100% power, we could shave about four hours off of our flight time. You know, make up some of what we've lost."

Dusty sighed inwardly, thinking, "This guy is really in a hurry."

"Well, Colonel, 100% is just a theoretical value. Because of mechanical inefficiencies, it's impossible to attain. The most we could get out of these power plants would be about 85%. And if we did that, our speed would increase a little, but our fuel consumption would increase a lot."

"And why is that?" Kittering asked skeptically.

"Because a little more speed means a lot more aerodynamic drag. It would be like stepping on the gas and the brakes at the same time."

"I see," Kittering replied dubiously. "Well it was just a suggestion, but I hope, Captain," Kittering went on pointedly, "that you appreciate the urgency of my mission."

"I do, Colonel. We'll get you there."

"I have every confidence in you," replied Kittering gruffly as he abruptly unfolded himself from the co-pilot's seat and walked away.

Dusty didn't know what Kittering's mission was. When he inquired, Kittering told him bluntly that he did not have the need to know, adding that further inquiries would be unwelcome.

Kittering had come aboard back at McGuire accompanied by a captain and two lieutenants. All four were wearing .45 caliber Browning automatic pistols in shiny leather holsters. The two lieutenants also carried Thompson submachine guns. The 15 courier bags were locked and sealed. Instead of being placed in the belly compartment, the bags had been strapped down to the floor in the passenger cabin under the watchful eyes of the gun-toting couriers.

It was not unusual for couriers to fly on cargo aircraft, but Dusty had never seen a situation where an entire flight had been used for that purpose. It was even more puzzling that high priority medical supplies like penicillin and blood plasma had been bumped from the flight. Such a thing was unprecedented. Dusty had no doubt that someone with a lot of influence had a high regard for Colonel Kittering's mission.

"A/C to Engineer."

"Yes, Captain," Pop responded immediately over the intercom.

"Ask Dan'l to come back up here, and if the navigator isn't too busy tell him I'd like see him also."

"Wilco, sir."

"How's that number two engine doing?"

"No sweat, Captain. All four are singing my song."

Smilin' Jack climbed down from his stool under the astrodome. He had gotten a good 3-star fix on Capella, Dubhe, and Sirius. Northern twilight still lingered, but those stars were so bright that he was able to get an acceptable fix on them even though it was not yet full dark. Plotting the fix on his chart, he was pleased to see that *Sky Queen* was on course. The wind, however, was stronger than forecast. His calculations showed the wind to be 23 knots, a ten-knot increase. Well, as the old saying went, "happiness is a tailwind." He worked out a new ETA and was preparing to call Dusty when Pop appeared at his shoulder.

"Cap'n wants to see you, Lieutenant."

"Okay, tell him I'll be right up."

"Radio, A/C," Dusty spoke into the intercom.

"Radio," Tex answered.

"How's your reception?"

"Getting worse, sir. I can still communicate with St. Johns on HF, but it's pretty noisy. I can hear a few other stations, but they're garbled."

"How about the low frequency stuff, the navigation beacons?"

"I can hear the identifiers for Stephenville and Reykjavik, but the radio compass is unstable. Mostly the needle just wanders around."

Dusty didn't like the sound of that. "Well, stay on top of it. Lieutenant Carter may ask you about the nav beacons. Also let St. Johns know about all these problems."

"Roger that, sir."

During that exchange, Dan'l had returned to the flight deck and taken his seat. Smilin' Jack was right behind him.

Dusty pointed to the co-pilot's control wheel. "Take over for a while, Dan."

"Now, what about this sunspot activity, Jack?" Dusty asked.

"I think it's going to be a problem. I got a pretty good fix with my last star sight, so I know where we are and what our groundspeed is. The stars are starting to get dimmer, though. I think that cloud layer at 25,000 is starting to thicken. I may not be able to shoot the stars much longer, so I've started a dead reckoning plot."

"Dammit!" Dusty fiddled with the cord from his throat mike and looked out his side window into the darkening sky. "Troubles are like bananas; they come in bunches."

"Yep. Murphy's Law, I guess."

"We'll be overtaking that next weather front in a couple of hours. It's forecast to extend all the way to England and probably beyond. You'd better take all the star sights you can before that happens."

"You know, Dusty, this situation can get out of hand in a hurry. Have you thought about returning?"

"Yeah, I thought about it, but if this mission is as important as I think it is we'd better make every effort to carry on. Colonel Frazzlebottom has already been up here complaining. Let me know when we reach PNR."

PNR—the Point of No Return. Jack had always thought that phrase to be overly dramatic carrying overtones of doom and disaster. It simply referred to that point in the progress of any flight where there was insufficient fuel to return to the point of origin. Your only choice then was to continue to your destination or to a viable alternate. Jack could see no viable alternates until they reached Ireland. By the time they got to Iceland, Reykjavik would almost certainly be socked in with weather. Well, in some respects that made his job easier. Jack had the feeling that this was going to be a long night. What the hell could they be carrying that was so all fired important?

Meanwhile, Dusty was thinking along the same lines, sifting through the various scenarios that might arise. Fuel and load, wind and weather, equipment and crew, mission and responsibility, the age-old problems of command tumbled over and over in his mind. Well, he had a good ship and a good crew. They wouldn't let him down. Good old reliable C-54. *Sky Queen* wouldn't let them down.

Dusty's thoughts were rudely interrupted by the urgent sound of his co-pilot's voice.

"We're picking up ice, Skipper!"

There are two words that no aviator wants to hear, and Dusty had just heard one of them. He grabbed his flashlight from its holder over his head and played it along the left wing's leading edge. Ice was forming on the wing, engine cowling, and most likely the propeller blades too. The windshield in front of him was already opaque. They had obviously entered a moisture-laden cloud. The outside air temperature gauge read 31 degrees.

"I've got it, Dan," Dusty said as he took hold of the control wheel and switched off the autopilot. "We're going to climb while we still can. A/C to crew, go on oxygen. Pop, switch on the deicing boots and shoot some alcohol on the props. Then go back and help our passengers with their oxygen equipment."

The ship was still heavy with fuel, and ice was adding more weight with each passing minute. She climbed sluggishly. Moreover, ice was altering the shape of her precisely engineered wing. She was losing lift. This was potentially serious. If the wing stalled and the Queen fell into spin, it would be the end of the line for them all. If the wing did not stall and they kept accumulating ice, *Sky Queen* would be forced down soon. The temperature of the water below was probably in the high 20s. Any crash survivors would have about four minutes to deploy the life rafts and climb aboard. These were not happy prospects.

Dusty shined his flashlight over the left wing again. The deicing boots weren't working! Under the sheet of clear ice, the black rubber deicing bladders were clearly visible. They should be pulsing, breaking the ice. There was no movement that Dusty could see.

"Pop!" Dusty called over his shoulder, "Are the deicers on?"

"Affirmative, sir."

"Well, they aren't working. Check it out."

"Wilco, Captain."

Sky Queen continued to claw sluggishly for altitude. The airspeed was falling. It was already down to 100 knots. *Queen* would stall at about 80 knots. The engines were straining, gulping fuel. Something would have to give–and soon!

Dan'l called out, "Captain, I think we're reaching the top of the cloud."

Dusty looked at the altimeter. It read 13,800. Well, that was a partial blessing, but *Sky Queen* couldn't mush through the air all the way to Ireland. The extra drag and weight from the ice required extra power, and was eating into their fuel. Dusty decided to level off at 15,000.

"Pop, how about those deicers?"

"Working on it, sir. The fuses are okay, so there must be a leak in the system somewhere. It'll take a few minutes to check."

"Well, hurry it up," Dusty said with exasperation. He regretted the comment as soon as he made it, though. He knew that Pop was doing his best. He'd apologize later.

Dusty had leveled off, set power for cruise again, and was trimming the ship when Pop appeared at his shoulder.

"I can't find anything wrong, Captain. The pumps just aren't working."

The two men looked at one another, trying to think of something they might have overlooked. After a few seconds, Pop said excitedly, "Wait a minute. I just thought of something," and disappeared.

A few minutes later, Dusty heard a noise outside the cabin. He looked out of his window and, miraculously, the deicer boots were working. Huge chunks of ice were breaking away, some of it being slung against the fuselage by the props. *Sky Queen* responded like a wet dog shaking water from its coat. Airspeed began to build and the controls lost their sluggish feel. Dusty noticed something else. The ice was actually melting. Water was streaming off of the wing and engine cowlings. He glanced at the outside air temperature gauge and was surprised to see that it now read 38 degrees. They must have climbed into warmer air–a temperature inversion!

Pop appeared at his shoulder again. "I found the problem, sir. It was the fuse after all. It looked good when I checked it visually, but it must have been defective. I replaced it with a spare, and the system seems to working okay now."

"That's welcome news, Sergeant," Dusty said beginning to breathe normally again, "Thanks a lot."

Dusty began to wonder if this trip was jinxed. Or was it something else. First there was the weather problem that had forced them to divert to Goose Bay. Then, the problem with the number two engine delayed them almost a full day. Now the icing situation and this mysterious problem with the deicing system fuse. Was all this just coincidence? He recalled a line from a spy thriller he had read recently, "Once is happenstance. Twice is coincidence. The third time it's enemy action." Dusty shook off the feeling. This was no time to let imagination run rampant. "Relax," he told himself, "It's only pressure causing your mind to play little tricks. There are no gremlins aboard this ship." He half believed it.

All was serene for the next several hours. Sky *Queen* droned eastward, her engines sounding as sweet as ever.

"A/C to Navigator."

"I'm right here, Dusty."

Jack was at that moment engaged in plotting what would probably be his last celestial fix. Higher clouds had prevented his getting the stars he wanted, but he did get a shot of the moon, the planet Mars, and the star Betelgeuse. It was a poor combination, and Jack wasn't happy with it. The fix indicated that they were still on course, but that groundspeed had increased another ten knots. Jack was skeptical. He settled on 30 knots, blaming it on the poor quality of the fix.

"You'd better get a fix pretty soon, Jack"

"I just finished one, Skipper. We're running ahead of the flight plan but still on course. I'll work out another ETA and let you know."

"Great." Then after a short pause Dusty added. "Everything else okay?"

Jack raised his eyebrows and wondered if Dusty was reading his mind.

"Yeah, I think so."

"Good. Give Tex your new ETA and have him notify Nutts Corner Radio; that is, if he can raise them."

"Wilco."

"By the way, how's our fuel?"

"That encounter with the ice used up some extra fuel, Skipper, but we'll be okay if we don't run into more problems."

"Fine. Oh, one other thing Jack. When you have a few minutes tell Colonel Kittering we're running ahead of schedule. Maybe that will keep him out of my hair."

"Okay," Jack replied laughing.

At that moment, Sky Queen entered solid clouds.

ARRIVAL

They had been on instruments off and on since the icing incident. At the moment, *Sky Queen* was enveloped in cloud. The weather had deteriorated further.

"Skipper, this is Jack."

"Go ahead, Jack."

"If my estimated ETA is anywhere near right we should be over Prestwick at 1150 Zulu. At that time, turn right to a heading of 167 degrees. That should take us to Blackbush. I've been using dead reckoning for quite a while now. I'd like to try for a celestial fix. Suppose we climb and try to get on top."

"I don't think so, Jack. I believe this stuff goes way on up. I don't want to use the fuel."

"Well, okay," Jack replied dubiously. "We haven't had an altimeter setting in quite a while, and Scotland has mountains," Jack warned.

"Yeah, Jack, I know. Go see Tex and have him start trying all frequencies. Maybe he can raise somebody. Meanwhile we'll stay at 15,000 for another 45 minutes. At that time, we'll start a descent and try to find the Irish Sea."

"Okay, Dusty, you're the boss."

Tex was still scanning the voice frequencies listed in his information for the British Isles. His ears actually hurt. All he could hear were irritating squeals, pops, and screeches. The Tower of Babel couldn't have been this bad. He had also tried all the navigation beacons with no joy. At one point he thought he had something. It was a faint signal that came and went. He was pretty sure that several times he had heard an identifier sounding like *dit dit dit…dit dit dit…dit dit dah dit…dah dit dit dit.* That was Morse code for Sugar, Sugar, Fox, Baker–SSFB. The problem was that no such beacon was listed in his frequency manual. He had no idea where SSFB was.

Then Tex had a disturbing thought, "I wonder if it's a Kraut station?" He knew the Germans sometimes transmitted false signals in an effort to lure the unwary into a trap. After thinking about it for a minute or so, he put it out of his mind. It didn't matter anyway. All he was receiving was the identifier. The radio compass needle still swung in lazy circles as it had maddeningly for the last eight hours or so.

"A/C to Radio. Any luck yet Tex?"

"No joy Skipper. I've found nothing on either the voice or nav freqs. I'm still trying."

"Okay, let me know when you get something we can use."

"Wilco, sir."

"A/C to crew. All right, listen up people. We're descending now. The Irish Sea should be below us somewhere. The first person to see anything will sing out loud and clear. Got that?"

Each member of the crew responded affirmatively. Dusty set the power for a 750-foot per minute descent, and they started down: 14,500...14,000...13,500...13,000 and so on. From the relative safety of altitude, *Sky Queen* swam earthward. Dusty leveled off momentarily at one thousand feet.

"Anybody see anything?"

A chorus of "no joys" and "negatives" followed.

"Okay, I'm going to descend a little more. Keep a sharp lookout. I don't know how accurate our altimeter is."

They started down again, this time at 250-feet per minute: 900...800...700. Slowly they descended. Dusty stopped the descent at 250 feet.

"We're not going any lower. This weather probably goes right down to the deck," he announced as he set climb power again.

Calling the navigator on the intercom, Dusty said, "Jack, I'm going to try to climb out of this stuff. You be ready to shoot something when we break out."

"When we break out? Boy there's the power of positive thinking at work," Jack thought to himself.

"Roger that, Skipper. I'll be ready. Meanwhile make your turn to 167 four minutes from now."

"Okay, Jack."

"A/C to Engineer. Pop, this climb will take a while and will be hard on the engines. Monitor the cylinder head and oil temps closely. Adjust the cowl flaps as necessary, but keep them at an absolute minimum. We don't need the extra drag."

"Okay, Skipper."

Sky Queen climbed upward, ever upward. About 1,000 feet per minute at first, but with an ever decreasing rate as she climbed into the thinning air. Eventually, she reached 25,800 and the big plane began to mush. There just weren't enough molecules of air to hold her up. Dusty pushed her on: 25,900…26,000…26,100. He felt the first shudder of a stall.

"That's it Jack. That's as high as she'll go."

"Wait a minute Skipper," shouted Jack excitedly, "I think I see something. Yeah! Hold her right there for one more minute."

It was a long minute. The *Queen* was straining every fiber of her being.

Finally, Dusty heard Jack say, "Okay, I've got it. Descend to a more comfortable altitude, but stay as high as you can. I'll have this worked out in a few minutes."

The star Jack had seen was Regulus, in the northern sky. A one-star fix would only give him a line of position, a single line. Their location would be somewhere on that line. He read the angle from his octant, consulted his navigation tables, and plotted it on his chart. Jack stared at the chart in disbelief! "That can't be right," he said to himself, "It just can't be!" Jack rechecked his work. The data was accurate. My God, they were somewhere over German-occupied territory! Damn, they must have picked up one helluva tailwind! He quickly spun his E6B flight computer. His eyes widened as he read the result. In his years as a navigator, Jack had never even heard of a tailwind that strong.

"Skipper, this is Jack. Turn back to the west. Fly a heading of 285. Descend to 5,000 as quick as you can. We're over occupied France, maybe Belgium. Don't descend out of these clouds. We might get shot down!"

Dusty was stunned. They had flown well past England! Instead of being near Blackbush where they should be, they were now somewhere over Western Europe. His ship was full of highly classified material that might be vital to the war effort, and they were over enemy territory! More than that, the icing problem and the long climb from sea level to 26,000 feet had used up a lot of extra fuel. Would they have enough to get to Blackbush? Dusty set the power for a descent, turned to the recommended course, and called Jack.

"Okay Jack, what the hell happened?"

"We picked up an unbelievably strong tailwind. It might have been the jet stream, that's why I recommended the descent. The winds will be much weaker down low. We now have a headwind, and I can only guess at its strength. I'm estimating about an hour back to the Channel."

Dusty had read somewhere about a mysterious river of air at the higher altitudes. Bomber crews flying B-29s at 30 to 35,000 feet had first reported it. The weather people thought that it moved north and south with the seasons and changed altitude seemingly at random. Nobody seemed to know much about it. It had simply been labeled "the jet stream." Also, no one had ever encountered it at 15,000 feet or any altitude as low as that before. They were in trouble, that much was certain. He decided to get closer to the Channel before breaking the news to Kittering.

Sky Queen droned on for the next forty minutes. Dusty brooded. Then looking at his watch, he called, "A/C to Engineer, engines okay?"

"Still singing sweetly, Captain."

"Well thank God for Pratt & Whitney. Ask Colonel Kittering to come up here right away, please."

"Wilco, sir."

"…and that's the whole story, Colonel," Dusty confessed. "Now what I need is for you to reach into your black bag of tricks and pull out a usable radio frequency. I know you've got one in there somewhere."

"Can we get to England?" Kittering asked with a deeply furrowed brow.

"Maybe. The question is can we find a place to make a landing that we can all walk away from."

"Have you got a VHF radio on board?"

"Well sure, but that's new technology. We don't have reference to VHF circuits over here."

"I've got one," Kittering said pulling a small white card out of his shirt pocket, "but they will only talk to me. Can I make the call from up here?"

"Right, sir. Standby."

"A/C to Radio."

Tex answered with, "Still no joy on those frequencies, Captain."

"Never mind that, Tex. Fire up the VHF Comm radio, and dial in…stand by."

"What's the frequency, Colonel?"

"One-one-seven-point-zero"

"Tex?"

"Right here, sir."

"Dial in one-one-seven-point-zero. Got that?"

"One seventeen nothing. Got it, sir."

"Good. Now rig an extension up here to the flight deck so that Colonel Kittering can talk on that circuit. I need that right now."

"It'll only take a minute, Captain."

A few minutes later, Colonel Kittering spoke, "Foxhunt, Foxhunt, Foxhunt, this is Jehovah. Over."

His transmission was followed by silence.

"Foxhunt, Foxhunt, Foxhunt, this is Jehovah, how do you read? Over." This was also followed by silence.

Rhodes and Kittering looked at each other with growing dismay.

"Foxhunt, Foxhunt, Foxhunt, if you read Jehovah, please answer. Listening on one-one-seven-point-zero."

Immediately a curt, authoritative response came over the frequency with, "Identify yourself. Over."

Rhodes and Kittering looked at each other, their eyes widening and grins starting to form on their faces. The Colonel recovered quickly.

"Foxhunt, this is Jehovah. I say phonetically; Jig, Easy, How, Oboe, Victor, Able, How. Over."

"The same voice came back with, "Stand by." This was followed a minute later with, "Say phonetically first and last letter of Jehovah's last name. Over."

"King-George. Over."

"Say Jehovah's service number. Over."

Kittering grinned at Dusty. "I think we're in."

"Foxhunt, Jehovah's service number follows: Oboe one-niner-eight-one-niner. Over."

After several nerve wracking minutes had passed, a different voice came over the frequency with, "Jehovah this is Killer. Identification confirmed. We've been worried about you. Where are you and what do you need. Over."

"We think we're over France. We have been out of radio communications for over ten hours. Have experienced unusually strong tailwinds. We need a Radio Direction Finder Steer and the local altimeter setting. Can you help? Over."

"Affirmative. The local altimeter at Foxhunt is 29.76. We are not DF equipped, but we know someone who is. Our recommendation follows. Advise ready to copy. Over."

Kittering pulled a small leather-bound notebook and a gold fountain pen from his shirt pocket and replied, "Ready to copy."

"Our sources advise ceilings over most of the English Channel are 300 to 500 feet. When able, descend over the Channel to visual conditions and fly to the English coast. Proceed north along to coast to Upper Thetford RAF Station. It's a fighter base with a 2,800-foot runway located about 90 miles north of London. The runway is short, but they have RDF equipment. Contact Upper Thetford on 4330 kilocycles, that's four-three-three-zero. Their call sign is 'Piccadilly'. Transport to this headquarters will be waiting. Did you copy all? Over."

"Affirmative."

"Good luck. We'll open the bar when you get here. Killer out."

"Thanks, make mine scotch. Jehovah out."

"Well," said Dusty, "that's the first good news we've had in long while."

"We're not out of the woods yet, though," Kittering said.

"No, but I'm going to get us out of the woods, starting right now."

"A/C to Navigator. Jack, can you come up here with your chart?"

A few minutes later, Smilin' Jack wedged his way onto the cramped flight deck, a rolled chart under his arm.

"What have we got, Skipper?" he asked.

"How much fuel do we have?"

"Forty-five minutes, maybe a little less."

"Where is the Channel?"

Jack shrugged but replied; "I think we're over it right now."

"Okay, I'm starting a descent right now," Dusty said, reaching for the engine controls. "Colonel Kittering will brief you on our plan. He has a radio frequency. See that Tex gets it. I want him to dial it into the radio, but I'll talk to them from the flight deck. Tell Tex to set that up. The local altimeter is 29.76."

Without waiting for an acknowledgement, Dusty punched his intercom button and said, "A/C to crew, we're descending over the English Channel. Keep a sharp lookout. We're looking for water. Sing out when you see it. Here we go."

Sky Queen drifted down through the murky sky. The altimeter unwound monotonously: 3,000…2,000…1,000; 600…500…400.

"Skipper, I see whitecaps. It's the Channel," the co-pilot shouted excitedly.

Dusty quickly stopped the descent, set the engine controls for economy cruise, and trimmed the ship for level flight. Visibility was poor, but they were in the clear.

Dan'l shouted again, "Breakers! I see the coastline dead ahead about two miles."

"A/C to Navigator."

"Go ahead, Skipper."

"Jack, I'm turning north now to parallel the coastline. Let me know when you have a positive fix on an identifiable landmark."

"I'm way ahead of you, Dusty. There's an estuary off to the left there. It has a distinctive shape and matches one on my chart. If I'm right, we're about 60 miles south of Upper Thetford."

"Okay, that's it then."

"Piccadilly, Piccadilly, this is Army 1734. Killer says hello. How do you read? Over."

A cheery English voice came back immediately. "I say, nice of you chaps to drop in. Your transmission is five by five. Piccadilly active runway is 27. Wind is 280 at 10 knots. Altimeter is 29.80. Piccadilly ceiling is 300 overcast. Visibility is two miles in light rain and fog. Sorry about the weather. Give me a long count for RDF identification. Over to you."

Dusty counted slowly from one to ten and back to one again. "How's that, Piccadilly?"

"Smashing, old boy. Absolutely wizard. We have you at 45 miles on a bearing of 170. Turn slightly left to 345 degrees. When shall we expect you? Over."

"Standby, Piccadilly."

"Jack, did you hear that?"

"Affirmative, Skipper. Working it out now. Stand by."

After a short pause, "Dusty, this is Jack. ETA is eighteen minutes."

"Roger that, Jack."

"Piccadilly, Piccadilly, this is Army 1734. Our ETA your station is one-eight minutes."

"Jolly good. Call us in one-five minutes. Tea's up!"

"Thanks. Our altitude is 400 feet. Any obstacles on this course?"

"Only the raindrops, old boy."

"Thank you, Piccadilly. Army 1734 standing by."

Fifteen minutes later, Dusty called again, "Piccadilly, Piccadilly, Army 1734. Over"

"Army 1734, Piccadilly. Descend to 200 feet. The field should be dead ahead, about two miles."

"Roger, Piccadilly. We're coming in on a wing and a prayer."

"A/C to crew. Prepare for emergency landing. It might be a little rough."

"Piccadilly, Piccadilly, I don't see the field. Over."

"Tally ho! I hear your engines, old boy. You are bang on. I've just turned the runway lights to full bright."

"There it is, Skipper," Dan'l shouted, "off the left wing. We're out of position. Make a tight left turn. Dammit, there goes the number four engine."

"Feather it, Dan! No time to fool with it."

Dan'l punched the number four feathering button and the propeller slowly wind milled to a stop. Meanwhile, Dusty shoved the mixture controls to full rich and hit the bar under the switches that would turn on all four electric fuel pumps. He doubted it would help, though. All fuel gauge needles indicated empty tanks.

Dusty craned his neck to keep the precious runway in sight while banking the *Queen* as steeply as he dared. Just as the runway came around to his two o'clock position, the number three engine quit. The runway was now dead ahead, about half a mile.

"Feather that one, too. Gear down! Flaps down!"

Dan's hands flew like a concert pianist as he punched the number three feathering button, shoved the landing gear lever all the way down, and hit the wing flap control.

Hydraulic pumps whined and the bumps and grinds of complex machinery filled the cabin as the landing gear rumbled down. The *Queen* groaned as she sailed over the end of Runway 27, her wheels clearing the fence by scant feet. Dusty hauled back on the control wheel and *Queen's* main gear crunched onto the short runway.

"Flaps up," shouted Dusty, "and get on these brakes with me." Just then the number one engine quit, its carburetors starved for fuel. *Queen* yawed violently, while the brakes and wheels screamed and smoked. The two pilots fought for control as the distant fence came rushing toward them.

Dan'l yelled, "The tires are probably going to blow."

"Just stay on those brakes," Dusty shouted. "Push as hard as you can."

Sky Queen slowed gradually, too gradually it seemed. Just as Dusty was thinking the United States Government was going to have to buy Piccadilly a new fence, *Queen* came to a shuddering stop at the end of the runway.

Dusty and Dan were breathing hard, as if they had just run a 400-meter foot race. Their shirts were soaked with sweat. Dusty managed to say between gulps of air, "Thanks, Piccadilly. Thanks for getting us here."

Piccadilly's voice came cheerily through their headphones. "I say, Yank, that rang the bell, but a bit of a dicey do. Are you all right?"

"I think so," Dusty answered quietly. At that moment, the number two engine sputtered and died. They were out of fuel.

CROSS COUNTRY FLYING[1]

I'll not believe but they ascend the sky,
And there sample God's gentle-sleeping peace.

—William Shakespeare

---

1. The two stories in this section were taken from a previously published work
   by the author.
   Helms, David. *Hawk and Me*. New York: Writers Club Press, 2000.

High Flight to Leadville

Sees God in clouds, or hears Him in the wind

—Alexander Pope

HIGH FLIGHT TO LEADVILLE

On the way to the field, it was evident that this would be a good flying day. The Lamar, Colorado, airport was equipped with an automated weather station. As I passed through the deserted terminal, I heard the ASOS over the station's receiver singing its litany of numbers:

> *Lamar Municipal Airport Automated Surface Observing System, one-three-five-one Zulu weather: no clouds below one-two thousand, visibility greater than one-zero, temperature six-one, dew point five-four, wind two-four-zero degrees at zero-four, altimeter three-zero-three-four.*
>
> *(Translation: Lamar Municipal Airport weather at 7:51 AM: the lowest clouds are at least 12,000 feet above the ground, visibility is greater than ten statute miles, air temperature is 61 degrees, dew point is 54 degrees, surface wind is from the southwest at four knots, local altimeter setting is 30.34.)*

The format was standard and quite familiar. Even the voice was the same no matter where the service was found. I only had to copy the information. It provided the essential advice for departure: sky conditions, visibility, temperature, dew point, wind direction and velocity, and the altimeter setting. These were "the numbers," so critical to safe flight.

I was keenly aware that this was the first day of what would probably be several weeks of mountain flying. So, I knew that I'd better get into the habit of computing density altitude. Density altitude is not really an altitude at all, but rather is a theoretical value upon which to predict airplane performance. To find density altitude, you take pressure altitude, what your altimeter would read if set to standard pressure of 29.92 inches of mercury, and correct it for non-standard temperature. The result is a measure of how "thick" or "thin" the air is. As density altitude *increases*, aircraft performance *decreases*. Here's a simple way to think of it: density altitude is the altitude the airplane thinks it's flying at.

Lamar's field elevation of 3,704 feet translated to a density altitude of 4,415 feet with the current temperature and pressure. That altitude wouldn't bother *Hawk*[1] at all. There was, however, a challenge coming.

Today we would visit Leadville, Colorado, high in the Rockies west of Denver. The airport at Leadville has the highest airport elevation in the United States: 9,927 feet!

Being early June, the temperature at Leadville would most probably be warmer than standard, so the density altitude when we arrived would likely be high also. I was not totally without mountain flying experience. I'd flown in the Western states half a dozen times or more and landed at many high altitude airports. Airports such as Bryce Canyon in Utah (7,586), Colorado Springs (6,184) and Durango (6,685) in Colorado, Grand Canyon in Arizona (6,606), and Santa Fe in New Mexico (6,345) had felt *Hawk*'s wheels. However, 9,927 feet was a daunting prospect for any pilot, let alone a "flatlander."

The Leadville landing and its subsequent takeoff had been on my mind for some time. I'd spent many hours reviewing mountain-flying techniques and high-density altitude operations. I'd studied the performance charts in *Hawk*'s *Pilot's Operating Handbook*[2] over and over again. Theoretically, there was no problem. Lake County's runway was 6,400 feet long, and I'd learned that the local Fixed Base Operator (FBO) flew standard C172s from there. However, experienced mountain pilots flew those airplanes, and they were stripped of all unnecessary weight. I wasn't worried, but I had to be careful. There could be no winging it (pardon the pun). This landing had to be "by the numbers."

Before beginning the ritual of the pre-flight inspection, I stood by *Hawk*'s nose and looked around, drinking in the beauty and peacefulness of the plains of Eastern Colorado. It was Sunday morning, and the airport was quiet. The entire field lay deserted except for *Hawk* and me. There were no airplane engines, fuel trucks, or any of man's noisemakers violating the sanctity of the moment. The only sounds came from birds calling

---

1. The aircraft the author calls *Hawk* is a 1978 Cessna R172K Hawk XP II, N736SL.
2. The *Pilot's Operating Handbook* (POH) is rather like the owner's manual for an automobile. However, it is much more comprehensive and filled with tables, charts, and graphs that predict airplane performance at various power settings and atmospheric conditions.

to one another and a slight whisper of wind in the grass. A movement caught my eye. A lean, gray coyote trotted across the sparse, brown grass near the windsock. The animal sniffed the air warily but paid me no mind.

The orange windsock hung almost limp, its big end pointing southwest and its small end moving slowly back and forth in the light, morning air. Overhead, there was a startlingly blue sky punctuated here and there by a few high clouds. Sixty-one degrees the system had declared a perfect morning temperature. I enjoyed quiet moments such as these in aviation. If God had thought more about it, He would have decreed that we hold religious services outdoors, on His land, under His sky, surrounded by His living things.

I was wearing my battered and beloved A2 leather jacket. I didn't really need it, but it was comfortable and easier to wear than to carry. Inside, it stated, "US Army Air Forces, Equipment, Flyers Type Garment" in the curious way the military had of describing things. I'd often wondered if somewhere on a computer tape or disk there was an entry next to my name reading: "US Air Force Person, Airman, Male." Probably so.

Shaking off my reverie, I set about my pre-flight chores. "Clear the prop," I shouted to the morning. *Hawk*'s power plant came quickly and eagerly to life. Allowing a few minutes for the engine to warm, I let idling power take us to the departure end of Runway 18, less than a quarter mile away, warming the engine more in the process. All four runways were available, but with little wind and no traffic I had chosen the nearest one.

The weather promised a rare day for flying. It was as near perfect as I had ever seen it. "A good day for VFR," (visual flight rules) I thought. I would navigate as the old timers had, using only my two eyeballs and the three Cs–chart, clock, and compass. Today we would have fun, *Hawk* and me. Let's go!

Hawk lifted easily into the smooth, morning air, using only a little more runway than usual because of the altitude. A right turn took us to the initial course of 270 degrees, exactly due west. Six minutes later we crossed the John Martin Reservoir, a 12-mile long bulge in the Arkansas River. At its western end was the river itself, a set of railroad tracks, and US Highway 50. They all led to Pueblo, our gateway into the Rocky Mountains.

As *Hawk* climbed to our initial cruising altitude of 8,500 feet, I saw the visibility was indeed greater than ten miles. It was actually closer to 70 miles! From our position east of Pueblo, the Rockies took definite shape. At first, they appeared as a smudge on the horizon, then as clouds. As we got closer though, the mountaintops became discernible. And then, there they were! The majestic Rocky Mountains rose in front of us like a great barrier rising out of the flat plains of Eastern Colorado. One distinctive, snow-capped mountain caught my eye at two o'clock and about 75 miles, Pike's Peak.

Several years ago *Hawk*, my wife Andrea, and I were on a flying vacation in the West and landed at Colorado Springs Airport about 40 miles northwest of Pueblo. We rented a car and drove the 20 or so miles to Pike's Peak. There is a Federal Aviation Regulation stating that pilots cannot fly higher than 12,500 feet for more than thirty minutes without using supplementary oxygen. Pike's Peak is 14,110 feet. Since I don't carry oxygen on board the airplane, I'm fond of telling friends that we drove the car higher than we could fly the airplane. Strange, but true.

In the distance, the city of Pueblo sparkled in the morning sunlight. I knew from a previous trip that, although Class D rather than Class C airspace surrounded the Pueblo Airport, there was an approach control facility located there. Being above that airspace, there was no regulatory reason to seek its services, but this pretty morning had attracted a gaggle of Sunday fliers. For that reason, I contacted Air Traffic Control and asked for traffic advisories until we were well within the valley beyond. ATC cheerfully obliged.

My old friends, the highway, railroad, and river, crawled out of the western edge of Pueblo. They formed parallel paths pointing the way for us, beckoning. All we had to do was follow, for they too were going to Leadville. At Canyon City, the valley made a slight dip southward for the next 35 miles, forming a shallow V on the chart. The weather was so nice that I decided not to follow the valley but to continue straight on to the town of Salida. The name means "exit" in Spanish, but for us it was the entrance to the glorious Rockies. This direct route took us over the higher terrain between Burned Timber Mountain and an unnamed peak soaring to over 11,000 feet. The Sangre de Cristo Range was at ten o'clock and 30 miles. *Hawk* climbed to 10,500.

The weather remained perfect. The weather gods, after punishing us for the last three days, had granted a reprieve. If the weather had not been so fine, I wouldn't have taken this little shortcut. Yet, cutting a few miles off the flight was not the point. The truth was I wanted to experience the feeling of flying in the mountains out of sight of civilization. There would be plenty of opportunities for that later in the trip, but I didn't stop to think of that. Meanwhile, the scenes through the cabin windows were so stunningly beautiful that my mind was almost overwhelmed with the splendor of the moment.

The first thing I noticed after leaving the valley was how close to the ground we were at our 10,500-foot altitude. The contour lines on my sectional chart showed that most of the terrain below was at the 8,500-foot level. Therefore, our actual altitude was only 2,000 feet above the ground. There were times, however, when we were only 500 to 1,000 feet above it, about traffic-pattern altitude. Individual trees and even individual branches on some of them were clearly visible.

The second thing was a sense of aloneness and detachment. There was no sign of civilization and there wouldn't be for a while. I'd even abandoned ATC, for my altitude was too low to converse with or even receive the controller's transmissions. I would feel this emotion many times throughout the remainder of this journey. Curiously, it wasn't trepidation or even uneasiness (or maybe only a little), but rather it was a sense of strangeness, of peaceful solitude. In our ordinary lives, we cannot divorce ourselves so completely from civilization and its icons. Most of us have never done so. The feeling of strangeness, I believe, stemmed from this detachment. It was oddly refreshing and fulfilling. Maybe somewhere inside me there was a little radio sorely in need of receiving nature's transmissions.

At Salida, we picked up the Arkansas River again and turned northwest up the valley leading to Leadville. As we flew on, the mountains grew higher and more numerous. Off the left wing was the Sawatch Range. On the chart, I counted more than a dozen peaks with elevations over 13,000 feet, most of them over 14,000 feet. The highest visible peak was Mount Elbert (14,433), and further northwest was Mount Harvard (14,420). All were snow-capped and appeared as giant inverted marshmallow-topped cones.

As we passed the airport near the small town of Buena Vista, I was surprised to see its runway was 8,300 feet long. Even at these elevations, that was a long runway for such a small town. The runway looked new. I wondered what was going on down there. I planned to make a fuel stop at Buena Vista on the way back. That way, *Hawk* wouldn't be heavy on departure from Leadville's high-altitude airport. I could check it out then.

Fifteen miles south of Lake County Airport, I called in for an airport advisory: traffic, altimeter setting, and temperature. I needed these last two items to calculate the density altitude. The calculation revealed 10,950 feet! Wow! All right, here was the moment of truth. With no reported traffic, I set up for a straight in landing on Runway 34. I used normal approach speed and just enough power to control the rate of descent. The ground speed would be higher than normal, so I set full flaps on short final and maintained a little power to cushion the landing.

Hawk gently kissed the asphalt and with gentle braking we turned off the runway at mid-field. The landing was so normal, so straightforward and anticlimactic that I hardly knew we were down. It was "no sweat" as we used to say in the air force or, as our British counterparts would say, "a piece of cake." I allowed myself a moment of quiet satisfaction. Flight instructors in primary training instilled in me the axiom, "Set it up right and it'll turn out right."

The parking ramp at Leadville was quite small, and there were only a couple of buildings on the field. They consisted of two hangars with an office shack attached to one of them. White letters painted on a hangar door proclaimed "Leadville Lake County Airport, Elevation 9,927 feet." Adjacent to the office shack stood two forlorn, rust-stained fuel pumps. On the barren rocky area between the ramp and the runway (there was no taxiway) stood an old horse-drawn farm wagon. It clearly had been placed there to give the airport a rustic look, as if such were needed.

Stepping down from the cabin, I stopped to look around. The first things to catch my attention were the buildings themselves. They were unpainted and had a heavily weathered look about them. There was almost no vegetation, only rocks and bare earth. The 10,000-foot level was clearly a harsh environment most of the time.

But as I raised my eyes to look out across the valley, I saw why a person would want to live here. Overhead, the sky was a deep blue, almost black, and contained no clouds. Its azure canopy came right down to the mountaintops and contrasted starkly but pleasurably with the dazzling pure white above the snow line. Below that, the medium to dark-green colors of the evergreens accentuated here and there with the gray of exposed granite swept down into the valley floor.

The air was so pure that I could almost taste it. It had sweetness about it, devoid of the pollution that most of us breathe daily. It also lacked moisture or particles of anything for it to condense on. Consequently, there was nothing to obstruct my vision on that marvelous Sunday. Only the mountains and the curvature of the earth restricted my view. The scene was probably equally magnificent during the fall of the year, or any season for that matter, when God's grace adorned the valley.

Reluctantly turning from the mountain loveliness, I entered the fuel shack to be greeted by a smiling young lady. After a friendly "howdy," she asked if this was my first trip to Leadville. Receiving an affirmative reply, she pulled from her desk drawer what appeared to be a certificate of some kind and began filling in the blanks with my name, aircraft number and the date. She explained that upon landing for the first time at Leadville, the FBO awarded pilots an embossed Certificate of Pilotage proclaiming:

> *This is to certify that (pilot's name) has navigated the airways of the Rocky Mountains and flown to North America's Highest Airport that overlooks the nation from an altitude of 9,927 feet.*

I was proud to have one with my name on it.

While I chatted with her, two guys walked in and asked to borrow the courtesy car or crew car as they are sometimes called. Many FBOs keep one or more cars around as loaners for transient pilots to use for local transport while visiting. The rules are simple: put gas in it and don't keep it too long. Occasionally, though, one can obtain use of such vehicles overnight as transport to the lodging facilities. Introducing myself, I asked if I could accompany them downtown. They had just flown in from Colorado Springs.

Interestingly, they were flying a Cessna T-41, the military version of the Hawk XP. Yes, it was another Hawk. The flying club to which they belonged acquired it from the Air Force Academy where it had been used as a primary trainer. I had flown the type in the Civil Air Patrol back in my search and rescue days and was familiar with it.

The primary difference between the Hawk XP and the T-41 was that its power plant had not been de-rated to 195 HP, as had the Hawk XP's. Rather the T-41 retained the full 210 HP. Also the T-41's nose wheel was larger, being the same size as the main wheels. Further, it did not have wheel pants and was not nearly so beautiful an airplane as *Hawk*, but no flying club airplane could be. I did, however, pick up several tips from them concerning high-altitude leaning technique.

After a short while, we rattled on up to town—it was about 600 feet higher than the airport—in the FBO's old VW Rabbit. The town had a weather-beaten, but orderly, look about it. Many of the buildings were constructed of wood, and some of those were unpainted. One did not have to look too closely to see that, as at the airport, this was clearly a harsh environment most of the year. That day, however, the weather was sunny with the temperature in the high fifties, cool but pleasant. Also, it was immediately apparent that there was an oxygen deficiency at this altitude. Walking around Leadville's hilly streets soon had me huffing and puffing.

The principal reason for the town's existence was mining. The town hosted a mining museum and diorama. The presentation showed the history, tools, techniques, and lifestyle of the mining industry in Leadville. If one has an interest in mining or just looking for an offbeat experience steeped in Western lore, this is the place. Also, the FBO offered a mountain-flying course that looked interesting.

After a quick sandwich the three of us returned to the airport, said our good-byes, and I began my departure preparations. The windsock showed the wind still favoring Runway 34. While taxiing, I reviewed the takeoff procedures. The main thing was to lean the engine properly in order to obtain maximum power. Having burned about two hours of fuel since Lamar, *Hawk*'s takeoff weight was well under the maximum. For high-density altitude operations, it is preferable that airplanes carry as little weight as is feasible.

I aligned the nose with the runway centerline, held the brakes firmly, set the wing flaps at ten degrees, pushed the throttle and propeller controls full forward, reduced fuel flow with the mixture control to that specified for the altitude, and released the brakes. The Continental sang its song in perfect pitch and harmony. *Hawk* was airborne by the time we'd used a quarter of the runway. I glanced at the vertical speed indicator and hardly believed what I saw. We were climbing at 450 feet per minute. The airplane couldn't sustain such a rate once the flaps had been retracted, but it was impressive.

At 11,500 feet, we were barely 1,500 feet above the ground. Incredible! The ground began to fall away, though, as I picked up the reverse course taking us the 26 miles to Buena Vista with its field elevation of only 7,945 feet (only?).

At Buena Vista Aviation's fuel pumps, the ramp guy greeted me pleasantly. "Top both," I said brightly as if ordering a ticket to some exotic destination, which indeed I was. While thus engaged, he noticed that the small chain securing the fuel cap to the neck of the left wing's fuel tank had come undone. "Not to worry," he said, "I will fix it for you." I love it.

Making small talk, I asked him about the new runway. He replied that the county was attempting to attract businesses, tourists, and sports enthusiasts to the area. So the town–together with the FAA and probably the State of Colorado as well–invested the money to modernize and enlarge the airport. The runway was now long enough to accommodate jet aircraft, and there was a fine new terminal building. Interestingly, it housed an art gallery.

Art galleries are not exactly standard equipment on airports. The extensive collection consisted mostly of Western and wildlife pieces. Local and regional artists exhibited their paintings and other works of art throughout the two-story building. Paintings, sketches, drawings, and sculptures occupied every bit of wall space. The art and motif were definitely Western.

After fuel for *Hawk* and a snack for me, we were off for Santa Fe. At Salida, we entered the narrow, ten-mile-long Poncha Pass (9,010) whose far end opened into the San Luis Valley. The valley was formed by the Sangre de Cristo Mountains to the east and the San Juan Mountains to the west. The mountains were high, mostly over 10,000 feet. Many peaks were over 12,000, with some over 13,000 at the north end. The valley was big, stretching southward for several hundred miles with an average width of about 35 miles.

Santa Fe lay near the valley's southern end. The valley floor was about 8,000 feet near Poncha Pass decreasing to about 7,000 feet at Santa Fe. Gone was the smooth, delightful air of the morning, though. The atmosphere, or more accurately the troposphere, had warmed, and we were flying in moderate turbulence. It wasn't dangerous, just tiring. I resolved myself to a long, two-hour flight. An axiom in aviation is that the length of a flight is directly proportional to the amount of discomfort to be endured.

Twenty-five miles northeast of Alamosa we came upon the Great Sand Dune National Monument. The dunes were tucked under the mountains to our left, shimmering in the light slanting across the valley from the western sky. At Alamosa, we picked up the famous Rio Grande River angling into the valley from the high terrain northwest. I would have missed it except for the name on the chart. It looked small, but when joined by the Rio Chama at Espanola it widened significantly.

The San Luis Valley possessed a kind of wild, western beauty. The colors were pleasing, with the earth tones of the West dominating. The deep-blue, cloudless sky and the huge, green circles indicating cultivation on the valley floor accentuated and lent interest to the scene. All would have been serene were it not for the irregular "slam-bang" of thermally induced turbulence. Pilots, it seemed, must always have something to complain about.

Eighteen miles northwest of Santa Fe and twelve miles off our right wing lay Los Alamos, where the Nuclear Age matured. Something was still obviously going on there, for my chart showed a 20-square-mile restricted area surrounding Los Alamos. The chart also showed a 5,500-foot private airport with a paved runway nearby. There are not many private airports in this country with paved runways, especially those with lengths over a mile. Something told me that we would not be welcomed visitors.

The Santa Fe ATIS advised that the wind was out of the southwest at eight knots with a temperature of 84 degrees. Calculating density altitude, I found that it was almost 9,000 feet on the ramp. No sweat, we'd just come from Leadville! We landed uneventfully (the best kind) at 1530, and I was pleased to see that "Connie" was home.

One of the first things one noticed when landing at Santa Fe's Municipal Airport was a Lockheed Constellation—or "Connie" as they are affectionately known—parked on the ramp north of the tower. This type was one of the mainstays of the world's airlines throughout the 1950s. No one seemed to know much about her except that she belonged to a local resident and she sometimes flew. She apparently was part of a collection of airplanes from bygone days owned by that individual.

A Constellation is truly a beautiful ship, perhaps the most beautiful ever designed. The fuselage has a distinctive, curvaceous shape. From her slender nose section to the perky upsweep of her tripletail, the aircraft is positively sensual. Having just visited an art gallery, I reminded myself that machines could also be works of art. If so, then a Constellation certainly qualifies. At rest on her tall, stately, landing gear she appears to be in motion. She wants to fly.

Another noticeable aspect of the airport, indeed the entire town, was the Indian and Spanish architecture. Nearly everything in this old Southwest city resembled one or the other. Even the control tower and buildings comprising the two FBOs, Santa Fe Aviation and Capital City Aviation, were designed to resemble adobe structures. Zoning laws protected and perpetuated the flavor of the Spanish and Indian cultures. Those cultures were an integral part of Santa Fe's history dating from the sixteenth century.

This delightful Old Spanish city is charming and unique. Santa Fe and nearby Taos are also havens for artists. Many art galleries are scattered throughout Santa Fe, and Taos is just one great big art gallery. Santa Fe deserved more of my time than I could give on this trip. But fortunately, I'd spent time here before. It used to be on my cross-country instrument training route: Atlanta to Paris (Texas) to Santa Fe to Colorado Springs to Dodge City to Little Rock and back again.

One of the most enjoyable meals I can remember was right here in Santa Fe at the Coyote Café. The name may sound like a lunch counter, but the Coyote was a first class restaurant. An immaculate, white table-cloth covered the table. An artful, desert arrangement graced its center. Waiters in black trousers and white shirts with black bow ties served a Southwestern meal with polished professionalism. There was even a wine steward. While this may sound a little stuffy, the entire experience was one of elegance, spiced with just the right touch of Southwestern informality.

It had been a long day, and *Hawk* and I needed sleep. Tomorrow we would fly further into the arid Southwest, over the Mogollon Rim, to Arizona's Zane Grey Country.

New York and a Patch of Fog

The bird let loose in eastern skies

—Thomas Moore

NEW YORK AND A PATCH OF FOG

We were in Danbury, Connecticut. It was Tuesday and time for *Hawk* and me to go hunting for adventure. The guy at the service counter at Reliant Aircraft, one of the airport's many fixed base operators, expressed an interest in my project. "Are you going down through New York City?" he asked rather casually.

The thought of going through or over the city had crossed my mind, but only briefly. The prospect of navigating through the busiest airspace in the world under visual flight rules at an altitude low enough for sightseeing was, I thought, too daunting even for one as adventurous as I. Filing an IFR flight plan wouldn't work either, because I knew that the New York controllers would simply vector me away from the city and out of their hair. My plan was to go over to Morristown, New Jersey, and proceed south toward Washington, thereby going around the New York Class B airspace altogether.

Looking at me curiously he asked, "Why would you want to do that?" When I explained my concerns, he told me that all I had to do was to get into the VFR corridor and fly straight through the city. "How do I do that?" I asked. "There's nothing like that marked on the chart."

"There's nothing to it," he replied opening a copy of the New York sectional chart and pointing at the Danbury Airport. "Here's where we are. Fly southwest until you come to the Hudson River at the Tappan Zee Bridge. Follow the river at or below 1,000 feet. The river will take you straight through the city. At the Statue of Liberty you'll be in New York Harbor. Look for a large bridge five miles further on. That'll be the Verazzano Narrows Bridge. New York Bay is beyond that and beyond that is the Jersey shore. What could be simpler?"

"What about a clearance?" I asked.

"You don't need a clearance as long as you stay over the river and under a thousand feet. ATC really doesn't care what you do down there. That's uncontrolled airspace." He had fanned the flames of my curiosity. Boy, this is going to be wild, I thought. Little did I know.

The weather on that July morning was a little hazy, but was VFR. The Danbury Airport's Automated Terminal Information Service (ATIS) called it 5,000 broken with visibility five miles in haze. I thought visibility would most likely improve as the day wore on, so I decided in favor of the proposed plan. Friends on the ramp waved goodbye as *Hawk* and I took off and climbed out of the bowl containing the Danbury Airport. I leveled off at 2,500 feet, intercepted the 240-degree radial from the Carmel VOR navigation station, and we were on our way to Broadway.

The distance from the airport to the Tappan Zee Bridge was 25 miles. The visibility aloft was better than five miles, probably closer to ten. Having departed Danbury at 1003, I anticipated seeing the bridge or the river by 1017. The bridge appeared out of the haze, on course and on time. I was surprised by the size of the Hudson. It was a larger river than I expected. It looked to be about two miles wide at the Tappan Zee Bridge.

The Hudson's headwaters are in the Adirondack Mountains. It flows 315 miles south and west to New York Harbor. Passing Troy, the equally famous Mohawk River–the Hudson's principal tributary–unites with it in a lazy journey to the harbor. The Hudson flows through spectacular countryside. The Roosevelt's estate at Hyde Park is on the Hudson. Also, the United States Military Academy at West Point is located 18 miles upriver from where we joined it.

West Point began life in pre-Revolutionary days as a military fortress. It is strategically sited on high cliffs on the river's western shore. These cliffs, called the Palisades, extend down river for another ten miles or so. The Hudson's width where we intercepted it is attributable to a lake-like bulge in the river called the Tappan Zee. The word *zee* is Dutch for sea. So far, the flight was progressing nicely.

The George Washington Bridge was 13 miles down river from the Tappan Zee Bridge, so we came upon it quickly. Arriving at the bridge, I saw the ghostly forms of the Manhattan buildings in the distance. How quickly we had found the city. Sometimes things happen too fast in an airplane.

Shortly, we came upon the Borough of Manhattan. I'd been there many times, so I was familiar with all the landmarks: the Empire State Building, the Chrysler Building, and the twin towers of the World Trade Center. The green expanse of Central Park slipped by under the left wing. The New York docks where great ocean liners once tied up were close abeam, with the aircraft carrier *Intrepid* immediately below us. I idly thought that I could probably land on its angled deck if it weren't for all the tourists. The Statue of Liberty sat in the harbor ahead. It seemed quite small surrounded by so many larger things.

I had earlier asked New York Approach Control for traffic advisories even though I didn't have to. The controller said that he could help but only if I stayed between 1,000 and 2,500 feet. I settled on 2,300 feet for a better visual perspective and to remain clear of the helicopter traffic constantly whop-whopping up and down the river. The higher altitude also provided a 200-foot cushion from the 2,500-foot level. The controller had previously told me to turn right to a heading of 220 degrees at the Statue of Liberty. All elements were now in place for another of those tense incidents that can come upon you so suddenly and unexpectedly when flying.

Since intercepting the river I had simply become a tourist, a sightseer. Only a small part of my conscious mind was concerned with following the river and maintaining altitude. Those actions were almost automatic. I was gawking at the scenery and not concerned with what lay ahead. I was committing the unpardonable sin of "falling behind the airplane."

At the Statue of Liberty I made the slight right turn requested by the controller and looked down at my chart to see where the new heading would take us. The controller wanted us to fly us across Staten Island to the Colt's Neck VOR just a few miles inland from the Jersey shore. Okay, that would work. As I dialed the VOR frequency into the number one navigation radio, something in the windshield caught my attention. Good grief! Fog! Where in heaven's name had that come from. One minute we were in visual conditions, and the next we were rapidly going into instrument weather. And here we were in the busiest airspace in the world. I began a mad scramble to catch up.

First, *fly the airplane*, so goes the basic rule of flying. Add this to it: *aviate, orientate, navigate; climb, confess, communicate, comply.* All right, first things first. I had to think, and quickly. *Hawk* was flying straight and level (good); we were heading south, away from all of New York's high obstructions (good); I could maintain orientation relative to the Colt's Neck VOR that thankfully I had already set in the radio (good); according to my chart, we were 500 feet above nearby obstructions (good); okay, it was time to talk to ATC.

Upon confessing my predicament, I told him I needed an IFR clearance to Cape May–now! He responded immediately with, "Roger, I'm working on it. Maintain VFR." *Yeah, right.*

"Seven Three Six Sierra Lima is proceeding direct Colt's Neck to hold at 1,000 feet," I said.

"That's uncontrolled airspace, and you're below my minimum vectoring altitude. Proceed at pilot's discretion. Maintain VFR," he responded.

The controller's last message indicated that he was concerned about my obstacle clearance. My chart, however, told me that as long as I stayed at or above 800 feet within a ten-mile radius of Colt's Neck that we were in no danger. That was no trick for an instrument pilot in an airplane with *Hawk's* modern navigation equipment. But I didn't want the controller to know I wasn't worried. I wanted him to work on my clearance, now. We weren't out of the woods yet.

The controller must have had to do quite a bit of coordination, for it was a good ten minutes before he called back with, "November Seven Three Six Sierra Lima is cleared to the Cape May County Airport via direct DIXIE, Victor 229 PANZE, Victor 44 Sea Isle, direct. Climb and maintain 6,000. Fly heading 190."

Good ol' ATC had come through again. I read back my clearance and thanked the controller sincerely. After all, my inattention had brought on a situation that presented him with a problem that he neither needed nor wanted. The controllers were always there to help, though, and he seemed as relieved as I was grateful. I settled down to the business of configuring *Hawk* for the climb and getting my navigation house in order.

Reading this scenario you're probably wondering why I didn't just turn around when entering the weather, the old classic 180-degree turn. There were several reasons. First, I didn't know how quickly nor in which direction that weather was moving. Weather can move pretty fast sometimes.

Second, I didn't want to be flying into all that traffic back there nor in a direction that would take me toward obstacles. Visions of that infamous 1945 accident involving an Army B-25 came to mind. The highly experienced pilot, finding himself in a similar situation, flew the airplane directly into the side of the Empire State Building. The resulting crash killed him, another crewmember, a passenger, and ten people in the building. Forget that! Finally, I wasn't familiar with the area and its special airspace rules and conditions. I figured my best course of action was to "get the hell outa Dodge." Right or wrong–and one can make a strong argument either way–it was my decision to make.

At 6,000 feet we were still in the soup. Patch of fog? This was no patch; this was a weather system. Why didn't my morning weather briefing warn me of it, you ask? It's because one of the things we know for certain concerning weather is this: Mother Nature doesn't always do what we think she's going to. I think it's just petulance on her part sometimes, sort of putting us in our place if you please. Nevertheless this wasn't the first time I'd seen such things, and it most likely wouldn't be the last.

DIXIE intersection was ten miles northeast of the old Navy airship base at Lakehurst, New Jersey, where the German airship *Hindenburg* mysteriously burned. Ten miles west of Lakehurst lay McGuire Air Force Base at Wrightstown. I had departed from McGuire for Europe in a C-118 during my service with the air force. July 1956, almost 40 years to the day. From DIXIE, our course took us south over the towns of Toms River and Waretown.

PANZE intersection was just east of Manahawkin near the Barnegat Light on the Jersey shore. From there, the course crossed directly over Atlantic City (did I hear the clink of slot machines?) and on into Cape May. The total distance from Colt's Neck to Cape May County Airport at Wildwood was 83 miles, about 45 minutes. We were still in solid weather. I saw nothing but the inside of clouds, so much for rubbernecking along the Jersey shore.

At last, the controller cleared me for the VOR approach to Cape May County Airport near the resort town of Wildwood. At the initial approach altitude, we were still in the clouds. Passing the Sea Isle VOR, I descended to the minimum descent altitude of 700 feet and saw the earth, but only straight down.

A few minutes later, the airport appeared out of the misty rain. Soon we were on the runway, the morning's adventure ended. I silently breathed a prayer of thanks to the Big Guy in the sky.

Cape May is a 10-mile wide, 25-mile long section of the southernmost tip of New Jersey. It juts southward into Delaware Bay, separating it from the Atlantic Ocean. The cape was named for a Dutchman, Cornelius Mey, who explored the region on the 1620s. Known for whaling in the eighteenth century, it has been a tourist and recreation area since the early nineteenth century. Too bad the weather didn't cooperate. I'd wanted to do a little exploring myself. It's probably pretty and restful here. Another day, perhaps.

The folks at Classic Air, the FBO, fueled *Hawk* while I enjoyed lunch: a granola bar and an apple. You were expecting soft-shell crabs and beer, maybe. No such luck. While so engaged, I wandered through a side door leading to the hangar area. There before my amazed eyes sat not one but–count 'em–two pristine North American P-51D fighters! There are precious few of these extraordinary aircraft still in existence, and to see even one is a rare treat. But to see two at one time was, well what can I say? It was exciting.

One of them had the name *Dixie* emblazoned on its long, slender, silver nose cowling. Remember my comment about the invisible navigation hand? DIXIE intersection had led us to *Dixie* the airplane, and tonight we'd sleep in Dixie. The other was in various stages of disassembly undergoing its annual inspection, so I could not determine its name. The airplane *Dixie* seemed so familiar. I'd seen it somewhere, some air show or other perhaps.

The mechanic told me that it belonged to a fellow named David Tallman. He's the guy who owns all the aviation theme restaurants: the 94th Aero Squadron, the 57th Fighter Group, the 101st Airborne, and probably others. For the aviation minded, they are pretty neat as restaurants go.

Better known as the *Mustang* and powered by that magnificent 12-cylinder, Rolls Royce Merlin engine, the P-51 owned the skies over Europe during the late stages of WW2. Not until introduction of this airplane would the heavy bombers of the US Eighth Air Force enjoy fighter protection all the way to the target and back. Not until then would the Allies achieve air superiority. I read somewhere that when the German Luftwaffe Chief Hermann Goering saw his first P-51 over Berlin he reportedly said, "Germany has lost the war."

Now it was time to go back to my war, a war with the weather. Millville Flight Service had encouraging news. While Delaware, Maryland, and Northern Virginia were still forecasting instrument conditions, the weather reportedly was improving to the south. Norfolk, Virginia, reported marginal VFR conditions and Elizabeth City, North Carolina, reported VFR conditions at the last hour. I filed an instrument flight plan to Elizabeth City. I wanted to be close enough to Kitty Hawk's First Flight Airport to make an early morning visit the following day. That's where the Wright Brothers Memorial and Museum are located.

Our route took us directly across the 12-mile wide mouth of Delaware Bay to the Waterloo VOR on the Delaware shore. From there, Airway V1 went to Salisbury, Maryland; Cape Charles, Virginia; Chesapeake Bay; Norfolk; and on into Elizabeth City. How many states was that? Let's see–Connecticut, New York, New Jersey, Delaware, Maryland, Virginia, and North Carolina–seven in all. The total distance from Danbury to Elizabeth City by our route, however, was only 340 miles. It seemed further than that.

The weather at departure from Cape May County Airport at 1300 was still instrument conditions. So I saw none of the immediate surroundings, the Atlantic Ocean, or even Delaware Bay itself. Leveling off at our cruise altitude of 4,000 feet, I cleaned up the airplane and resigned myself to a boring flight on instruments.

At 1347, Chesapeake Bay loomed out of the haze and mist of Pocomoke Sound. Visibility, while still not good, was definitely improving. Flight conditions were now merely marginal. We were flying down the west shore of Cape Charles. The cape is about 80 miles long with an average width of 12 to 15 miles. It separates Chesapeake Bay from the Atlantic Ocean, and actually forms the bay.

Looking westward, I could not see the mainland. It was over there somewhere, though, 20 miles away. The mouths of the Potomac and Rappahannock Rivers lay shrouded in the cloud, haze, and mist of the weather. They were also shrouded in the mist of history. The area between those two rivers was where Union General George McClellan bogged down his Army of the Potomac in the marshland. He was futilely trying to outflank Joseph E. Johnston's Army of Northern Virginia in order to capture Richmond early in the American Civil War. It was a major embarrassment for McClellan.

Even though the mouth of Chesapeake Bay was only 12 miles wide, our flight plan route took us over water about twice that distance. It would be the last significant body of water we'd have to cross. The weather continued to improve. Visibility was about eight miles as viewed from our 4,000-foot altitude. I relaxed a little.

Off the left wing I saw what appeared to be an unfinished bridge standing out into the bay from Cape Charles. As we got closer, there was a segment of open water and what appeared to be another unfinished span sitting all alone in the middle of the bay. I was curious and asked Norfolk Approach Control for clearance to fly over there and take a look. "Approved as requested," replied the controller.

About a mile from the "bridge," I finally realized what it was. This was the Chesapeake Bay Tunnel. Never having actually seen it, I had pictured it as a literal tunnel under the entire mouth of the bay. In actuality, it was a bridge/tunnel composite. A normal-looking bridge emanated from one shore for a few miles then disappeared under the water into a tunnel. After a few more miles, the tunnel reappeared as a bridge once again. It then disappeared a second time as another tunnel for several miles then reappeared as a final bridge to the opposite shore.

Thus from the air, one saw a 12-mile-long bridge with two gaps in it, each about two miles wide. Obviously this was done so that ships entering or leaving the bay would have two water gates, one for incoming traffic and the other for outgoing traffic.

The area inside the mouth of Chesapeake Bay is known as Hampton Roads. Somewhere under the water just off *Hawk's* right wing lies the CSS

Virginia, more often referred to as the *Merrimack*. Here, on March 9, 1862, the USS *Monitor* and CSS *Virginia* fought their historic duel. The calm and peaceful water below belied the savagery of that battle in an even more savage war.

We crossed the southern shoreline between two large airports near Norfolk. Norfolk International Airport was about five miles off the right wing with Oceana Naval Air Station about the same distance off the other wing. Eight minutes later, we crossed into North Carolina. Below lay nothing but swamp covering perhaps a hundred square miles. The chart labeled it "Dismal Swamp." Well, I suppose all swamps are dismal. This one certainly was, although it possessed a kind of wild and forbidding beauty.

The airport at Elizabeth City was a dual-use airport. The Coast Guard occupied one side of the field while the civilian operations were located on the opposite side. The Coast Guard ran the tower, with the runways being shared. There were two large C-130 transport aircraft in the pattern doing touch-and-go landings. "Caution, wake turbulence," the tower warned as I was cleared to land. Large airplanes at slow airspeeds leave a lot of energy behind them in the form of disturbed air. Wake turbulence has been known to throw small or even medium-sized airplanes completely out of control. We touched down on runway 10 at 1455, the end of another difficult but exciting day.

Elizabeth City, named for Queen Elizabeth I, is old. The city was first settled in 1650. Situated at the northwest end of the Pasquotank River, it is now the major port on Albemarle Sound. Kitty Hawk, on North Carolina's famed Outer Banks, is 28 miles to the southeast. That, however, was for tomorrow. At the moment, I just enjoyed that sense of homecoming that people feel when entering their home state after a prolonged absence. It was a comfortable feeling, rather like putting on an old sweater on a crisp, fall day.

The Poetry of Flight

A poem begins in delight and ends in wisdom

—Robert Frost

Lure of the Sky

The lure of the sky is strong, and
When the wind is in the trees we long
To go aloft.

Where there are freshening skies, and
Dew covers her wings we rise to greet
The breaking dawn.

The sky will free our soul, and we'll
Be made whole again in the
High blue silence.

For only in that quiet place can
We be completely at peace in
A troubled world.

Awaken, my craft,
And take me there.

Remember

Remember the October day we met? You looked odd in
Confederate gray, but no sweat. I knew we'd get along.

In the next few months through spring and fall we had
Such great times; we had a ball. What fun!

Then came the work. While I struggled to learn, how we
Suffered. But I found your every quirk and you found mine.

I'd thought myself a pilot, child that I was, tho' you knew.
My flaws made you frown, but onward we flew.

You showed the way thru clouds and rain and stood by
Me as together we rode the highways of the sky, laughing.

Then came paint of white and blue; Oh you were pretty, too.
No more Old Lady in Gray, though I always liked you that way.

You would always be "The Gray Ghost[1]." Whenever I wanted
You would take me to mountain or coast. You gladly flew.

Where do you soar now; what skies touch your wings? I wonder,
As your memory clings to my heart, and I grieve for you.

---

1. "The Gray Ghost" was a 1973 Cessna 172M Skyhawk, N20554. The aircraft
belonged to the South Seminole Flying Club in Sanford, Florida. She was
heavily damaged in a hailstorm and declared a total loss. The insurance
company sold her for salvage.

Fly no more, gentle lady. Fold your battered wings and sleep.
For whenever I hear an engine where there is no plane, I'll not weep.
But I will remember.

Night Flight

The ancient litany of the pre-flight ended
With the click, sharp and clear, of the
Master Switch.
"Clear prop," I shouted at the cold
December night[2], though there was
No one there to hear.

"County Tower, 96164 ready on 32," I said,
Requesting takeoff clearance from the
Man high in the tower cab, alone.
And those words, the essential but magical
Key to flight, came through my headphone.
"Cleared for takeoff."

The throaty Lycoming engine roared its
Song of power as it swung the big
Six and a half foot Hartzell prop.
And at her pilot's touch, skilful and light,
The T41 flying as "Redstar Flight"
Flung herself into the starry night.

Once again, the Civil Air Patrol had set out in
Search of a faint radio signal that could end
As so many others would–nothing more
Than the careless act of a thoughtless pilot.

---

2. The author was called from a warm bed one cold Atlanta night to fly a search
and rescue mission for the Civil Air Patrol. That experience resulted in
"Night Flight."

But one day that insistent sound would mean
Downed brothers and sisters in distress.

And those aerial volunteers, the Unsung Few,
Who willingly fly the demanding and often
Dangerous missions into the blue,
Would be there to stand between the
Unfortunate pilot, passengers, and crew
And an unwelcome date with eternity.

Enigma at Sea

'Twas whispered in heaven, 'twas muttered in hell,
And echo caught faintly the sound as it fell;
On the confines of earth 'twas permitted to rest,
And the depths of the ocean its presence confess'd

—Catherine Fanshawe

©1981 David Helms

ENIGMA AT SEA

It was cold on the North Atlantic that April night. The lookout at the foretop shivered, his eyes watery with the cold. He stamped his feet and thrust his hands deeper into his duffel coat. He desperately wanted a cup of hot tea to ease his misery.

Just a few minutes ago, he had heard the ship's bell strike seven bells—half past eleven. In less than thirty minutes his relief was scheduled to appear.

"Blimey, 'e better be on time this night."

He raised his eyes above the level of the steel windbreak at his station for another look ahead. For a few precious seconds his brain refused to believe what his eyes were telling it. He shook his head, rubbed his eyes, and looked again. This time he believed.

Its huge bulk soared above the surface of the cold sea, higher than a ten-story building, and it was several hundred yards across. It shimmered with a pale, ghostly, inner glow as if powered by some ethereal energy unknown to man. It made no sound, but crept in like Carl Sandburg's fog, on little cat feet. Was it really there? Yes, he could smell it. It smelled like— well it smelled like land. But it was not land. It was an iceberg!

He rang the alarm bell and screamed into his telephone, "Bridge there! Iceberg right ahead."

The captain had posted the ice watch after receiving reports over the new Marconi wireless that 'bergs were on the move. He had, however, decided not reduce speed. The last four days had been done in record time and the much-coveted Atlantic Blue Riband, awarded for the fastest cross-ing, was close at hand. It would be an impressive way to close his forty-two year career as a sailor. No, he would not give that up so easily. The night, though moonless, was clear, the sea calm, and he was in command of a well-trained crew and the most magnificent vessel man had ever built. The risk, he judged, was a small one. Before he retired for the night, he wrote in the ship's log, "Weather clear, course 235, speed 22, maintain."

With the lookout's cry still ringing in his ears, the duty officer shouted, "Left full rudder. All back full." Two things happened instantly. The quartermaster pulled the big levers on the engine room telegraph from "Full Ahead" to "Full Astern." Simultaneously, the helmsman on the big rudder control began to turn the ponderous wheel. Grasping the spokes at the top, he swung them all the way to the deck then reached back for another handful. His muscles rippled along his back and arms, sweat broke out on his body under his dark blue wool jumper. His breathing was heavy between grunts of exertion.

The rudder, though, was slow to turn. It was huge, weighing a full ten tons, and this was in the days before power assistance. Even though delicately balanced on greased bearings, it required twenty half turns of the wheel to traverse the full forty degrees from "rudder amidships" to "full left rudder." Even then, the 46,000 ton bulk of the ship moving at 22 knots, propelled by three giant screws each turned by 15,000 horsepower, required a great deal of sea room to avoid the impending collision.

"What are those bloody fools doing down there on the bridge?" shouted the lookout to himself. "Why aren't they turning the ship?"

"Bridge there! Iceberg now half a mile; distance closing rapidly."

The lookout did not fully understand the physics of the moment, but the duty officer did. He stared at the rapidly increasing size of the phosphorescent monster.

"My rudder is full left, sir."

"Very well. You there at the control board, sound collision alarm; close watertight doors. Signalman, call the captain."

"Aye aye, sir," they chorused.

The duty officer had not taken his eyes from the expanse of ice, but he was not transfixed. Rather, he was visually measuring the distance and rate of turn. Yes, the ship had finally begun to turn. She was turning slowly, but the rate of turn was increasing. Would it be enough?

"Report, mister." said a quiet voice.

"I believe she's going to clear the part we can see, sir," replied the duty officer, recognizing Captain Smith's voice, "but will she clear the part we cannot see?"

"I don't think so," replied the captain. The two officers stood together, awed by the mountain of ice ahead. The bow was swinging quite rapidly now, but the distance was closing with equal speed–five hundred yards, four hundred, three. The bow was clear now and still swinging–two hundred yards, one hundred, fifty. The bow was well clear now–thirty yards, twenty, ten.

Then they were moving past the 'berg. The smell of it was dank and eerie, like a graveyard on a wet and dewy night. It radiated cold like the bite of an arctic wind. It radiated death as well. The duty officer started to breathe again.

"I believe you're wrong, sir."

"Wait!"

Almost as the captain said the word, the ship shuddered. There was a screeching sound from somewhere below like the howl of a disturbed pack of banshees. Then the iceberg was behind them, slowly bobbing in their wake. The bright brass clock on the bulkhead behind them read 11:40.

The clock did not disclose it, but the date was April 14, 1912. Nor did it disclose the location, 95 nautical miles south of Grand Bank, Newfoundland. Nor did it, with all its timekeeping accuracy, disclose that RMS *Titanic*, pride of the famed White Star Line, had two hours and forty minutes to live.

How could this be? How could this wondrous ship, miracle of the age, zenith of the shipbuilder's art, said to be unsinkable, sink? The iceberg ripped a three hundred foot gash in her hull, low on the starboard side. The tear exposed six of her sixteen watertight compartments to the cruel sea. She was designed to stay afloat with any four compartments flooded, but this night she would die. Along with her, 1589 passengers and crew would die also. It would be a cold, lonely, bitterly hard death.

"Notify Mr. Andrews, the ship's designer. Give him my compliments and ask him to make an inspection, please. Also, ask the Chief Engineer to provide whatever assistance Mr. Andrews may need. Ask the Second Officer to make preparations to swing out the lifeboats. Have the Purser's Department wake the passengers." Captain Smith gave these orders quietly and professionally. He didn't yet know he was going to lose his ship. In his view these were merely precautions.

Huge chunks of the iceberg had fallen onto the main deck, and several crewmen and passengers had gathered around them. A few of the passengers began to push some of the smaller pieces around as if playing some strange hockey game. They were laughing, joking, and carousing as young men sometimes do. No one could envision that the *Titanic* would come to grief over such a seemingly insignificant event.

Two of the crewmen, George Seales and Robert Guardian, lifelong friends from Liverpool, stood idly by.

"I say, George, look at that chunk of ice there."

"Where?"

"Right there. It looks as if it has something buried in it."

"Ah, Go on with ye. It's just a shadow."

"It's nae a shadow, Georgie me lad. It's glowing."

Meanwhile on the bridge, the captain awaited the damage report. The minutes ticked slowly by as the *Titanic* drifted, all lights ablaze, still in the company of the iceberg with which it had so calamitously mated. What seemed like hours was actually only a matter of minutes. The captain saw, however, that they were in real trouble. The bow had already begun to sink toward the surface of the sea, and the ship had taken a slight list to starboard–all in less than fifteen minutes.

On a nearby bulkhead, a telephone buzzed urgently. "Bridge," the duty officer answered. "Yes, he's right here. Captain, it's Mr. Andrews."

"This is the captain speaking," Smith said quietly.

"I'm afraid I have bad news, sir. She's been badly hurt under the waterline," Andrews reported. "It's mortal. We're going to lose her." Andrews went on to explain the technical and physical aspects of the damage.

Ever the professional, Captain Smith did not argue with what his eyes had already told him. Almost absently, he looked through the bridge windows at the cold, leaden surface of the sea. He knew that many would die.

"How much time does she have?"

"An hour, sir, maybe two. Not much more than that."

"Very well. Thank you, Mr. Andrews. You'd better see to your safety," Smith said as if speaking to his own son.

"Mr. Duty Officer, have the wireless office send out a distress call. Report that we are sinking and require immediate assistance. Get our position from the navigator and add it to the message. Keep sending it as long as we have power. Alert all hands. Prepare to abandon ship."

Back on the main deck, the two lifelong friends were still staring at the chunk of ice.

"Are ye daft, man?" George said to his friend. "It can't be glowing. Whatever it is, it's been locked in that ice for a thousand years. It's just a stray shaft of light."

"You're the daft one. It's not only glowing, it's pulsing with a weird orange glow. It's right in front of your eyes man, something from another world I'm thinking," Robert said in awe and with considerable impatience.

"Let's break it out and carry it to the bridge. They'll know what to do with it," replied George, the more adventurous of the two.

"Better you than me, chum. 'Ere. 'Ere's me knife. 'Ave at it, laddie."

"Get out of it. I can use me own knife, can't I?"

With that comment, George began to chip away at the block of ice. After several minutes of hard work, the ice suddenly split open and something, now free from the ice, rolled onto the deck.

The object was round and no larger than a golf ball. George picked it up and hefted it. For its size, it was extremely heavy, weighing perhaps a pound or two. As he turned it over in his hands, he noticed the pulsing had increased and the orange glow was turning red. The object started to feel warm in his hands. Just as he thought he should put it back on the deck, the pulsing stopped. The color was now a deep, angry-looking red.

Suddenly, a shrill high-pitched sound pierced the cold dark night. The two men held their hands to their ears. Nearby passengers and other crewmen did the same. The sound was loud, almost painful. George dropped the object. It rolled under a nearby lifeboat, all the while continuing its shrieking. All at once a pale light surrounded the ship, followed by a brilliant flash of white. It was somewhat like lightning without the thunder.

On the bridge, a telephone buzzed urgently. "Bridge," the duty officer answered. "Yes, he's right here. Captain, it's Mr. Andrews."

"This is the captain speaking," Smith said quietly.

"Good news, Captain. It must be a miracle, but there's almost no visible damage. We have a minor leak in compartment number four, aft of frame 45. The pumps are taking care of it nicely. I see no reason why we can't continue at normal speed.

The captain suddenly looked younger. Care was leaving his bearded face when a startled cry from one of the bridge lookouts immediately brought it back.

"Sir, the iceberg is–it's sinking!"

"Wha-a-a-t? Why that's impossible. Let me see; let me through here!" the captain said loudly as he shouldered his way to the wing of the bridge.

The iceberg, forgotten for the past half hour in all the excitement, was indeed sinking. Unbelievably, it was almost submerged. Atlantic waves were breaking over its majestic crest. For a few minutes it lingered near the surface. Then, as if in a desperate effort to reverse the process, it lifted itself into the air and with an almost audible sigh it slid beneath the sea and was gone. On the opposite side of the ship, unnoticed by everyone, a small object flung itself from under lifeboat number seven. It silently streaked toward the stratosphere, leaving only a faint trail of multi-colored sparks.

No one spoke right away. Each was feeling a curious, unexplained sadness at the passing of what had been their only companion on the sea that night.

"Well," said the duty officer, "It's gone."

"Yes," replied the signalman, a youth of about nineteen. And for lack of something more profound to say, continued with, "and it was such a nice iceberg, too."

Others on the bridge began to roar uncontrollably with laughter, their pent up tension and emotion suddenly released. Captain Smith smiled and placed his hand paternally on the youth's shoulder.

"Full speed ahead, Mr. Duty Officer. Ring up turns for twenty-two knots and let's go get that Atlantic Blue Riband.

"Twenty-two knots it is, sir."

The *Titanic* began to pick up speed, her long curving wake indicating the turn that would point her bow to New York–and fame.

A Special Evening

Love does not consist in gazing at each other,
but in looking outward together in the same direction

—Antoine de Saint-Exupéry

A SPECIAL EVENING

Tonight will be special, and she is so beautiful, Andy thought. He was watching his new bride, Carol, as she stood before the mirror in the hotel room they'd called home for the past week. She knew that Andy was watching her, saw him in the mirror, but she pretended to be unaware of his attention. She was glad now that she had selected the sexy and intimate panties and bra he had given her, and that she had not yet put on her slip and dress.

"Honey, did you call for reservations?"

"Oh damn," said Andy reaching for the phone. "I forgot. "I hope it's not too late."

He thumbed the yellow pages to the restaurant section, turned a few pages, and then a puzzled look came over his face.

"That's funny, I don't see it here."

Carol turned to him with just a hint of concern in her eyes.

"Maybe they've gone out of business."

"Not a chance," he replied.

Carol watched him as he continued to search the yellow pages and then the white pages. Finally, as a last resort, he called Directory Assistance.

"Sorry, sir. Looking under restaurants I find no listing for *L'Italia*."

"Okay, thanks," he said placing the phone in its cradle. "I guess they've closed or something."

"Don't worry, darling. We'll find another one."

"I know, but I've been telling you about this place for days, and I deliberately saved it for our last night."

Andy really knows Washington, and he hasn't been wrong yet, thought Carol. She could see the disappointment spreading over his face.

"I guess we'll have to make another selection," Andy said thoughtfully.

"It's all right, my sweet," Carol said brightly. "Any place will be fine as long as we're together."

"Together, huh, now that's an idea," Andy whispered, hugging her from behind her back, his hands beginning to wander.

"Do you want to go out, or what?" Carol said, pulling away coyly.

"Well, maybe we should eat occasionally." They both laughed. It had been good so far–even magical.

"Alright, Darling, we'll have dinner at *Romeo and Juliet's* again. You liked that place."

"Well, it's certainly appropriate," Carol remarked, placing her hand on his cheek and kissing him softly.

Ten minutes later they stepped off the elevator into the lobby, and Andy saw a taxi pull up outside.

"Hey, we're in luck," he said over his shoulder as he ran for the door.

"Your carriage awaits, my dear princess," he said holding the door for her.

"Thank you, kind sir."

"Where to, Mac."

Andy looked at the driver and saw a wizened little man smiling at him with a rather crooked, knowing little smile. Strange little man, he thought. Also, the cab had a rather musty smell as if it had just come out of storage. The radio was playing a song that hadn't been popular for several years. Must be one of those "golden oldie" stations, Andy mused. Even the name on the side of the car, *Georgetown Taxi Service*, was unfamiliar. Funny, thought Andy, I don't remember this cab company.

"You folks goin' to dinner?" Their strange-looking driver asked.

"Yeah," replied Andy.

"Okay, where to?"

"We really wanted to go to a place called *L'Italia*," Carol said.

"But I guess it's not there anymore," Andy added.

"Oh, I think I can find it," their driver replied confidently with an odd smile, and drove off into the Washington traffic.

"Honey, maybe it is still there," Carol said, flashing Andy one of her beautiful smiles.

"Could be," mused Andy. "Say, driver, just where do you think this place is?"

"It's over in Georgetown near the old canal, ain't it?"

"That's right," replied Andy taking Carol's hand.

"We must be living right, sweetheart. The magic is still working."

"Yes Andy, and it always will," she replied, clasping his hand to her cheek lovingly.

Fifteen minutes later their driver announced, "Well, here we are, folks. That'll be three dollars and sixty cents."

"Thank you, driver," Andy said, handing him a five-dollar bill.

"Thanks, now you two have a pleasant evening," their driver said with that same odd smile, and he drove away into the night.

"Come on, Carol. This is it. I remember that little brass plaque on the side of the building with *L'Italia* engraved on it. Now, the next thing we have to worry about is reservations," he said.

"I wonder why they weren't in the phone book." Carol responded.

Andy led her through a quaint lobby filled with old world antiques, through an unmarked door, down a flight of stairs, and through another door with another small brass plaque reading *L'Italia*. Immediately, the quiet was broken by the hubbub of happy laughter and typical restaurant noises as they stepped into the crowded dining room.

"Oh. Andy," said Carol despairingly, "Look at all these people. We'll never get a table."

"Look!" said Andy.

Carol looked in the direction of Andy's eyes and saw a tall, distinguished man with silver hair, dressed in a tuxedo shouldering his way through the crowd, beckoning to them with an open smile.

"Don't look a gift horse in the mouth," Andy whispered out of the side of his mouth, grabbing Carol's hand and following the *Maitre d'Hotel*.

"Will this table be satisfactory, sir?"

"Sure," Andy replied grinning as the handsome, tuxedoed gentleman held Carol's chair for her.

"Cocktails before dinner, sir?"

"A White Russian for the lady, and I'll have a Black Jack and Soda."

"Very good, sir. Your waiter will be with you shortly. If there's anything you need just ask for me. I am Mr. Angelo."

"Wow, what service," Andy said as he looked at Carol admiringly. "Did I tell you how beautiful you are in that filmy green dress?"

"No, would you like to?" she responded teasingly.

"Yes, among other things," he smiled laughingly, following Carol's lead.

"Andy, did you notice that this is the only open table here?"

"Yes I did, and it looks like the best table for two in the entire room."

"Andy, there's something strange about this place, but in a warm and intimate way," Carol remarked looking around.

"Maybe, but it sure smells good. And did you notice, honey, there are fresh flowers of all kinds on the tables. Ours has a large, red rose. Now how could they have known that roses are your favorite?"

"Oh Andy, roses are everyone's favorite," Carol replied, cupping her hand around the single blossom and sniffing its perfume.

Not one, but two waiters served their exquisite meal. The food was tasty and delicious. The salads were fresh and crisp. The main courses, consisting of two different veal dishes, were exquisite. The wine put them in a warm and mellow mood, as good wine will. The desserts and coffee were to die for. The entire experience seemed out of this world.

Andy marveled at Carol. In all the time he had known her he had never seen her quite so excited. She couldn't sit still. Her eyes sparkled; her conversation was bright and witty, and best of all she appeared happier than he had ever seen her. From the corner of his eye, he saw that several nearby men had noticed, too.

"Carol, I think I see what you mean about this place being slightly odd. Even though the restaurant is crowded it doesn't seem to be unduly noisy. Furthermore, the waiters seem to come just when you need them and then disappear. It seems as if the entire place knows that this is our special evening."

"Yes," Carol replied, "if there were a graceful way to thank them, I would."

As they were leaving, Andy took the rose from its vase and handed it to Carol whispering huskily, "You know what red roses mean don't you?"

"Yes, they signify deep and abiding love, my love. Thank you for a perfect evening," Carol whispered back kissing his lips lightly. It's all so wonderful, I don't want to leave."

The following morning after a satisfying breakfast, they took a long walk before returning to the hotel shortly before noon.

"Well, we're all packed."

"Yes," replied Carol. "I don't want to leave, such beautiful memories."

"Hey, we've got a few hours to kill before our flight. Let's go back to that restaurant. Maybe they serve lunch or something."

"Oh darling, what a perfectly wonderful idea."

"Come on, let's hurry."

Andy and Carol rushed to the lobby; and as on the previous night, a cab pulled up just as they walked out onto the street.

"*L'Italia*, driver, and hurry."

"Where's that, sir?" the driver asked with a puzzled look.

"Why it's in Georgetown, down by the old canal."

"Ain't a restaurant by that name in this whole town, Georgetown or anywhere's else."

"Of course there is. We had dinner there just last night," Andy replied impatiently.

"Ain't a restaurant by that name in this whole town, sir," the driver said again stubbornly.

"Okay, just follow my instructions, and I'll show you where it is."

"Anything you say, Mac. It's your money."

As they rounded the corner twenty minutes later Andy said, "Well, there it is, looking at the driver rather than the spot where the restaurant was supposed to be."

"Ain't a restaurant by that name in this whole town," the driver said one last time.

"It's right there," Andy said, his voice rising.

But as he looked, his heart chilled and his brain reeled as a wave of disbelief flooded over him. Where the restaurant should have been, Andy and Carol saw nothing but a vacant lot upon which rested the remains of a fire-blackened building.

"Andy," Carol said fearfully, her eyes widening in shock. "What is this; what's happening?"

"I don't know. Let's get out and have a look."

The fire had obviously happened some time ago. Weeds had grown around the fire-seared timbers. Trash had accumulated in the wreckage, and dirt had built up in little windrows along the sidewalk like sand on a deserted beach.

"This can't be the same place, Andy."

"It can't possibly be, but it is," Andy replied in a quiet voice knowing full well that he had just said something totally preposterous.

As he poked around in the debris near what had once been the front door, his foot hit something hard and metallic. He reached down, picked it up, and brushed off the blackened dirt and corrosion. The word *L'Italia* formed under his fingers. Stunned, Andy and Carol could only stare at one another.

"Love, I'm frightened," Carol whispered clutching his arm.

Andy felt her body trembling. "Me, too."

As they stood there looking, feeling, experiencing–they knew not what– they were startled by a voice.

"Bad fire all right. Two years ago, almost to the day." Andy and Carol turned to see a bearded old man with a cane and a frayed rucksack over one shoulder.

"Were you here that night?" Andy asked.

"Yep, sure was a bad one."

"How did it happen?"

"Don't rightly know, son. Just happened," the old man said slowly, shaking his head from side to side.

"Was anyone hurt?" Carol asked with almost total fascination, not at all sure she wanted to hear the old man's answer.

"Can't say," the old man replied. "Don't know. Well, you folks have a real nice day now," the old man said quietly, shuffling off as mysteriously as he had come.

"I think we'd better go too, honey," Andy said, his voice quivering with emotion. "Let's get out of here."

As they turned to go, Carol exclaimed, "Look! Oh, Andy, look!" Andy turned in the direction of Carol's trembling finger. There, alongside a large, charred timber that had once been a main roof support, was a lovely, freshly cut, long-stemmed red rose. Andy picked it up and looked at it, turning it over and over in his hands thoughtfully, almost reverently. The eerie, uncomfortable feeling he'd had for the last ten minutes left him, and in its place there came a warm, peaceful sensation.

"You know," he said, "until this moment I wasn't sure what was happening. Now I think I do. Remember how we couldn't find the telephone listing, but found a taxi driver who knew exactly where we wanted to go? Remember how warm and happy everyone was? Remember, too, how they seemed to understand that we were in love and had eyes only for each other? Remember how there just happened to be one open table when we didn't even have reservations? Remember the waiters, the food and drink, how perfect everything was; just as if it had been created for us alone? Well, I think it was. Don't ask me to explain it. I can't. But I know that it was. This red rose proves it. Red roses symbolize true love, Carol. You said so yourself. That's what we have, and this experience proves it."

Andy placed the rose in Carol's hand, and with that touch he kissed her gently, sweetly. They joined hands and walked away from *L'Italia* toward their future, secure in the knowledge that it would be a bright and happy one. For as the rose survived the crucible of fire, Andy and Carol knew their love would survive the crucible of life.

THE HITCH HIKER

Say we not well that thou art a Samaritan, and hast a devil?

—John 8:48

©1957 David Helms

THE HITCH HIKER[1]

Matt eased the Mercury onto US Highway 1 and swung north. He shifted gears automatically and thought about the past five days. It had been a good week. He smiled and lit a cigarette. He was happy in his job, and he felt a glow inside him as warm and reassuring as the Daytona sun beaming down upon the bright ribbon of concrete stretching away before him.

He relaxed behind the wheel, running his fingers contentedly over its smooth surface. He never tired of hearing the powerful growl of the Merc's engine as it gathered momentum, hungry for speed. Yes, he was sure that this had been one of his best weeks ever. He grinned as he mentally tabulated the commission.

It wasn't until the gaudy roadside advertisements were flashing past him like flicking cards that the comfortable, contented feeling began slipping away from him, and in its place there grew the same nagging problem that had dogged him for months.

Matt was 28, and after serving a hitch in the air force, had tried several career fields unsuccessfully. Then AutoAcc hired him as a traveling salesman. Matt found that he had natural sales talent. He grew to love his work—two years of flashy chrome, weirdly shaped spotlights, hot rod gadgets, and ornate automotive novelties. He had thrown himself into the job night and day to become one of AutoAcc's most successful salesmen.

Diane could not understand that. She could not understand that in those two years wheeling around Florida, Georgia, and the Carolinas—wherever there was a chance to sell a mirror, a wheel cover, or anything chrome—he had been alive as he had never been before. He'd found his place in life and was happy with it.

He tried to understand her feelings. She wanted him home because she loved him. Matt suspected she was lonely, too. But more than that, Diane

---

1. "The Hitch Hiker" won First Prize at base level competition in the United States Air Force short story contest in 1957. The author was then serving with the Military Air Transport Service in Northern England. Winning with his first attempt ever, it began a love of writing that has continued to this day.

told him time and again that the children should have more than just a weekend father. Well, he couldn't argue with that.

He tried to change. A hundred times he promised her that he would look for something else. But he had never done it. He just couldn't. When he climbed into that blue Merc on Monday morning and waved goodbye, that old feeling would come over him and he would be helpless in its grip.

He would feel a sense of guilt because he looked forward to speeding into the labyrinth of work and wheels like Robinson Crusoe dashing to the valley of echoes to hear his own voice. The dry, hot roads beckoned to him like the Sirens calling to Odysseus.

Matt was wrecking his marriage, and he knew it. Lately, there had been a kind of cold aloofness in Diane's manner toward him. He was almost like a guest in his own home–an unwelcome guest at that. Matt had been indignant, angry, and hurt, but he knew that he had brought it upon him-self. If only she would understand. He pondered as the miles slipped by under the whispering wheels of the flashing Merc.

As Matt crossed the St. John's River, a clap of thunder shook him loose from his thoughts, and it began to rain–hard. He switched on the wind-shield wipers, and they flicked back and forth like the swords of Athos and D'Artagnan, bravely fighting off the enemy. He looked at the clock on the dash. He would be pulling into Jacksonville in a few minutes, and visions of Ma's ham and eggs and coffee pushed the problem from his mind. Soon he saw the red and yellow neon sign, *Ma Logan's Truck Stop*, flash a homey welcome through the lashing rain.

Janet Martin was despondent and tired as she sipped at her coffee in a booth at Ma's place. The current state of her life wasn't to her liking. At 23, she'd quit her boring job as a secretary and traveled to Florida to find a singing job in one of the swank nightclubs on Miami Beach. But it had not taken her long to realize that the men who wanted to hire her were interested in more than her singing. It was much the same wherever she went. They looked at her with that same leering look and spoke with that same sugary sweetness. Thanks, anyway. She was sure there was more to life than that.

Janet was not above using her looks to gain advantage. She knew she was pretty in a fresh and youthful way. She knew how to dress seductively, and her voice had a naturally sexy quality about it. Also, it usually helped if she smiled and leaned forward in her chair while being interviewed. That, though, was as far as her principles and virtues had allowed her to go. Now as she looked back on it, she wondered if she had done the smart thing. After all, principles and virtues won't feed you or keep a roof over your head.

But it was too late to do anything about that now. She had to think about the present. She had just spent her last nickel on the cup of coffee on the table in front of her and was now stranded. She would have to do something soon, but as she looked about the room at the rough, unshaven truckers, she shuddered. "Not one of those," she thought, cringing inwardly. "I just couldn't."

She looked out the window and saw that it had begun to rain. The rain spattered against the pane of glass at her booth and was instantly bathed in the multi-various colors from the neon lights on the front of the building. "Even the sky is crying tonight," she thought. Her spirits sank another notch.

Ma Logan sat behind her cash register and looked around her place with a critical eye, missing nothing. She liked what she saw. She had been running the truck stop ever since her husband died four years ago. It had not been easy at first. She had gone deeply in debt to redecorate and install new equipment in the kitchen and dining room. It had been worth it, though. Now, almost every trucker on the north-south run frequented her place. She was famous for her good, clean, wholesome food, the hallmark of every good restaurant. Her place was now a paying concern, and for that she was grateful. She was approaching sixty and was thinking and planning toward the day when she could retire.

Outside, it began to rain. Ma smiled to herself. "The place will be crowded soon," she thought. "It always is on a rainy night."

The jukebox blared forth endlessly and seemed to groan under the weight of its coins. Over the general hubbub, one of the newer arrivals was calling impatiently.

"Okay, keep your shirt on. I'm coming," said Ma brusquely, climbing down from her high stool.

As she passed the front window on the way to the customer's booth, she looked out and saw a car pull up in front. Even in the obscure wetness, she recognized Matt's distinctive blue Mercury. She motioned for a waitress to take care of the trucker's order and waited by the door for him to enter.

Ma's place was a regular stop for Matt when he was in Jacksonville, and they had become good friends. Ma was worried about him. For the last few months, he had not been himself, and she wondered what was bothering him. She had not inquired, however, for she was not the type to butt in on someone's private life without being asked.

Matt pushed through the door like a Georgia Bulldog fullback charging the line.

"Hi ya', Ma," he said, seeing her. "Boy this rain sure is somethin', huh?"

"Well, you don't have to break your neck getting out of it," she chided. "Now you just sit down right here and get your breath." She sat across from him.

"How're Diane and the boys?"

Something flickered behind Matt's eyes, but he answered: "Oh, they're just fine, Ma. The boys are growin' like–like boys, I guess."

I'm real glad to hear that, son. Now you just stay right here, and I'll get your special ready."

"I sure do look forward to eating at your place, Ma. Why I'd drive a hundred miles for your ham and eggs."

"Shucks, Matt, you flatter a woman in her old age."

"Not at all. You're the best cook this side of Washington." He winked at her and she blushed like a schoolgirl.

"I'd better get your food before you ask me to marry you." They laughed together.

Matt settled himself comfortably in his seat and looked around the steaming room. There was the ever-present group of truck drivers talking loudly to each other about baseball, road conditions, the cost of diesel fuel, and the virtues of various mutual female acquaintances. Against the wall sat the usual tourist couple, wise to the fact that Ma's place served the most wholesome food on the highway. His gaze finally settled on the lone girl sitting in a booth by the window. "Nice," he thought. "Very nice."

A few minutes later, Ma returned with a jug of coffee and a steaming platter of ham and eggs. As she placed the order on the table in front of Matt, he asked:

"Hey, Ma, who's that good-lookin' girl sitting in the corner booth?"

Ma looked at him curiously. She had never known Matt to express interest in other women before. "So that's it. He's having trouble at home." She followed his gaze to Janet's booth. "I don't know," she said. "She came in about an hour ago."

Janet looked up and saw them watching her. "This might be my chance," she thought. She mustered up her courage and smiled at Matt.

Matt had never been unfaithful to Diane in all of the seven years they had been married, but with the recent trouble still fresh in his mind, he figured Diane probably wouldn't even care. He got up and walked over to her booth. "Mind if I join you?" he asked giving her his winning salesman's smile.

"Please do," she replied, huskily. But Janet was shaking inwardly. She tried to control herself, for she did not want this man to discover that she was a novice.

Matt motioned to Ma to bring his order to the girl's booth. Ma looked at him disapprovingly, but she complied.

"Would you like something to eat?" he asked Janet.

"Maybe you'd better introduce yourself first," she replied, with an equally winning smile.

"I'm sorry. My name's Matthew Myers–just call me Matt."

"All right, Matt," she smiled. "I'm Janet Martin–Janet."

"How about some ham and eggs, Janet?"

"Sounds fine."

"Another order of ham and eggs, Ma."

"I hope you know what you're doin'," Ma whispered as she turned to leave.

"What's a pretty girl like you doing in a place like this alone?" Matt asked her, immediately regretting that he'd not thought of something more original.

"Well, as a matter of fact, I'm stranded. I was on my way home, and I ran out of money. I'm from Richmond."

"Well, I'm on my way to Charleston. Why don't you ride with me that far. I'm sure I can get you the rest of the way, somehow." Matt wanted her along as much for company as for the promise he could see in her eyes. It was a long ride, especially at night.

Janet appraised him, as women will do. There was something about Matt that she found attractive. He had blond hair, blue eyes, and a rather boyish charm. "Well," she thought, "I could do a lot worse."

"I'd love to, Matt." She said, flashing a warm smile at him, "It's sweet of you to help a lady in distress."

"Think nuthin' uv it, Ma'am. We Suthanahs ah noted foah ouah gallantry," he mocked, laughing.

Ma brought Janet's order, and Matt and the girl dug in ravenously.

When they had finished, Matt asked her, "Good?"

"Mmm, yes."

"Ready to go?"

"Well, just let me run to the ladies room. I won't be a minute."

"I'll wait for you up front," Matt responded as he got up to pay the check.

Ma was waiting at the cash register wearing a disapproving look.

"I wish you wouldn't do this."

"I know what I'm doin'."

"That's just the point. I don't think you do."

"'Bye, Ma. I'll see you next trip."

"'Bye, son."

In a few minutes, Janet joined him. Matt helped her with her coat, picked up her bag, and they hurried through the rain to the car. Ma gazed worriedly after them as they drove into the rainy night.

"Well, we're off."

"Yes," she answered quietly.

The rain hissed under the tires and the headlights bored a tunnel of brilliance into the night as the car sped northward. There was no moon because of the rain clouds, so the only illumination inside the car was the reflection of the instrument lamps. It was cozy and warm.

Janet was quiet at first. She seemed deep in thought, and Matt allowed her this privilege. It was not until they crossed the state line into Georgia that she seemed inclined to conversation.

"Where are we?" she asked.

"In Georgia," he replied.

"What time will we reach Charleston?"

"Mmm, let's see," he glanced at the clock on the dash. "It'll be a few more hours yet. Why don't you try to get a little sleep?"

"Are you sleepy?"

"Not yet."

"I'm not either."

Shorty Yeager urged the ancient Ford to the limit of its endurance. He sat hunched over the wheel as if by the sheer force of his will he could squeeze more speed out of her. The old car seemed to be cursing Shorty with its backfires and strange noises as it trembled and shook like a rodeo bull. Shorty gripped the wheel savagely. He was in a bad mood.

He cursed his bad luck and his stupidity. He hadn't meant to kill old man Brewster. All he wanted was the money that everyone said was in his mattress. He hadn't figured the old fool would put up such a fight. He hadn't figured on the old man's bad heart, either. The exertion must have been too much, because Brewster had died. No matter how you looked at it, it was murder. Shorty was in trouble—bad trouble.

Even the weather seemed against him. The rain had slowed his progress. Also, his tracks were all over the old man's place. A piercing tremor of fear ran through his vitals as he realized it wouldn't take the cops long to figure out who they wanted. Shorty's foot pressed harder on the gas pedal, and the old Ford shrieked its protest.

The worn tires seemed to sing a mocking song to him as they flapped over the highway–run Shorty–run Shorty–run Shorty. The expansion joints on the bridge rumbled as the Ford rocked over them. Thumpity—thump! Shorty left the bridge behind and careened around the next curve. Then it came. There was a sound like an explosion and the wheel jerked viciously in his hands. The car skittered over the highway, jumped the ditch, and landed in the adjacent field where it bounced to a stop. Shorty climbed out.

"Damn! A blowout," he cursed. He lit a cigarette and stood there once again blaming his bad luck. He lashed out viciously at the tired old car with his foot, but only succeeded in bruising his toes.

Shorty thought for a moment, and then a smile played momentarily over his ruddy features. He reached into the car and pulled out the bag containing the money and his few possessions. He flung a last curse at the old car and made his way toward the highway. In the distance, he could hear the faint hum of a powerful engine.

Matt glanced at the speedometer and was pleased. "We're making good time," he said to the girl beside him. "We'll be coming into Savannah in another hour, maybe less."

"That's fine," she said, but she had only a vague idea where Savannah was.

Janet was thinking about the unspoken pact she had made with Matt. She was sure that it was a mistake. She wondered what she would do when it came time to deliver. What could she tell him? Would she go through with it? Would he force her? These questions tormented her, and she was torn by indecision and doubt.

Matt, too, had been thinking about Diane and the children. What would they say if they knew what he was doing right now? He glanced at the girl beside him. "I wonder what she'll say if I don't go through with it," he wondered. "Well, whatever happens, I'll see that she gets home." Matt was reminded of a play that he had once seen about another salesman and the circumstances that led to its tragic climax. His conscience nagged at him.

The Mercury rumbled over a bridge, and the joints went thump-ity-thump. As they rounded the next curve, Matt saw the figure of a man outlined in the glare of the headlights. He was waving to them.

"Look, Matt," Janet said, "There's someone out there."

"I see him."

Matt usually picked up hitchhikers, but with the girl along he wasn't so sure. Still it was raining, and the man seemed to be in trouble. It was Matt's nature to play the Good Samaritan whenever he got the opportunity.

"I'm going to stop," he announced as his foot touched the brake.

"Do you think it's safe?" she asked worriedly.

"I've never had any trouble," he answered reassuringly "and he seems to be having difficulty. I wouldn't pass up a dog in this stuff."

Janet lowered her window as the car came to a stop.

"What's the trouble, Buddy?" Matt called as the man came alongside.

"I've had sort of an accident," Shorty replied.

"What kind of an accident? Was anybody hurt?"

"No, I'm traveling alone. A tire blew out and my car wound up in that field over there. I'll have to find a tow truck to pull me out. Can you take me to Savannah? I have friends there, and I can come back for the car in the morning."

"Sure thing," said Matt. "Hop in the back. What's your name?"

"Lester Stone," Shorty lied.

"I'm Matthew Myers. Just call me Matt—everybody does—and this is Janet."

"Pleased to meetcha, I'm sure," said Shorty.

"Well, now that we know each other, let's go." And with that, he eased the Mercury onto the highway once more.

"Do you mind if I catch forty winks back here?" said Shorty, not wanting to make any more conversation than necessary.

"Not at all," replied Matt.

"Let's have a little music," said Janet, moving closer to Matt. She thought her action was a bit like whistling past a graveyard.

Matt turned on the radio and tuned it to WCKY–Cincinnati.

"They only play hillbilly music on this station, but it's the only one that will come in clearly at this time of the evening." They sped through the night to the strains of "Good night, Irene."

Thirty minutes later, they reached Savannah and Matt stopped for gas. Janet left for the ladies room, and the attendant filled the tank.

"Where can I let you off, Les?"

"My cousin lives just on the north side of town. I'd be pleased if you would let me off there. It's on your way."

"Sure thing," Matt replied. He looked up and saw the attendant approaching.

"Check your oil, Mister?"

"No thanks, the oil's okay. How much?"

"Four dollars and fifty-seven cents," replied the attendant glancing at the meter.

"Here's a five. Keep the change."

"Thanks, Mister. Come again."

Five minutes later, they were cruising through the edge of town.

"Where is this cousin of yours, Les?"

"Never mind the cousin, Buster. This is a gun in your back. Just do as I say and nobody will get hurt. Keep driving."

"What kind of a game is this?" Matt asked, knowing full well that it was no game.

"This is no damn game, so shut up. No funny business or I'll put a couple of bullets in you."

Matt didn't like the tone of the man's voice. He thought it likely that this hitchhiker would not hesitate to shoot either of them.

"Don't get excited with that gun. We'll do as you say."

"You bet you will, if you know what's good for you."

Matt's mind reeled. He had been in tough spots before, but he had never experienced anything like this. His mind was filled with visions of Diane and his boys. How could he have betrayed them like this? Would he ever see them again? He was sure that he was being punished for the way he had neglected them. And this girl, Janet; what would happen to her? He shook off the ugly picture that question presented. She seemed like a nice kid–just a girl in trouble who had tried to help herself the only way she knew.

He glanced at Janet and saw that she was frozen, wide-eyed with fear. He cursed himself, and swore a silent oath. If he got out of this jam, he would make it up to all of them. He would take another job and be home with his family every night. They seemed so much dearer to him now.

Janet was terribly frightened. She had made a mess of her life, and now she was going to lose it. Well, she would be spared the future she had nearly entered. If only she had another chance, maybe she would be able to make a go of it.

Shorty sat grimly in the rear seat, clutching his pistol like a drunkard clutches his bottle. He did not realize it, but he was a catalyst in the lives of Matt and Janet, and he had already begun to take effect.

An hour dragged by. Matt glanced at the clock on the dash and saw that it was nearly midnight. There was no telling when the killer would grow tired of their company. He had to think of something, but what?

He looked at the rear-view mirror and saw the hitchhiker was awake and alert. On the seat beside Matt lay his order pad and a pencil. He filed this bit of information away for future reference. And then a thought came to him! If he could get the killer to lean over the seat…It was a hundred-to-one chance, but by God he was going to try it!

He let his right hand fall casually to his side and picked up the pencil lying there. He began to print in large letters on the order pad, hoping the light from the instrument lamps would allow Janet to read it. When he finished, he tapped her on the leg with the pencil. He was not looking at her, but he sensed she was watching him. He motioned toward the pad, hoping she would understand.

Janet looked down at the seat beside her and saw Matt's message scrawled on the pad: BRACE YOURSELF FAST STOP. She turned the pad over, and looked at Matt. She saw him reach under the dash. The instrument lamps dimmed.

"What's goin' on up there?" Shorty growled suspiciously.

"The engine temperature's rising, and the oil pressure's falling," Matt replied, allowing alarm to creep into his voice. "Something's wrong with the lights, too. Guess I should have had the oil checked back there."

"Let me see," Shorty said nervously. He leaned over the seat to look at the instruments.

Matt hit the brakes as hard as he could! He almost stood on the pedal. The car swerved and the tortured tires shrieked and smoked. Janet screamed. Shorty flew over the seat like a slug from a .45, and his head crunched against the dash with a sickening sound. He dropped like a sack of wet sand.

Matt called upon all his skill as he fought the wheel to keep the careening, skidding machine on the road. He finally managed to bring it to a safe stop.

"Looks like our boy is unconscious," he said, picking up the gun. "You all right?"

"I–I think so," Janet replied shakily.

"Can you drive?"

"I don't know. I–I'll try."

"Good girl."

Matt wrestled Shorty's inert form into the back seat and crawled in beside him.

"There's a highway patrol station about twenty miles further on. We can deposit 'Sleeping Beauty' there."

Janet eased the car onto the highway and drove slowly in the direction of the patrol station.

"After several minutes, she spoke. "Matt?"

"Yeah?"

"I want to tell you something, you know, about me. I'm not—"

"You don't have to say it, kid. I understand."

"You're not—"

"Don't worry about it." He smiled in the darkness. "Everything's going to be okay, Janet. It's all going to be just fine."

She said no more, but Matt sensed her feelings. Up ahead, a few lights blinked on the horizon. Somehow he knew, as the Mercury surged powerfully through the blackness, that Janet was smiling too.

Myths of Gettysburg

I can anticipate no greater calamity for the country than the dissolution of the Union. It would be an accumulation of all the evils we complain of, and I am willing to sacrifice everything but honor for its preservation

—Colonel Robert E. Lee, January 23, 1861

©2005 David Helms

MYTHS OF GETTYSBURG

Books written about the Battle of Gettysburg would likely fill a large warehouse. Probably the best of the fictionalized versions is *The Killer Angels* by Michael Shaara. The popular TV movie, *Gettysburg,* is based on this book.

In my opinion, the book is much better than the movie, although the movie is quite good. But one must keep in mind that neither are serious historical works. The book is reasonably faithful to history and does contain much truth. But it is a novel, and Shaara took literary license where necessary for dramatic effect. Since the movie was based on the book, its producers of necessity did the same thing–only more so. Neither Shaara nor the screenwriters need give apologies, though. After all, they are presenting entertainment, not history.

The book is so well written and realistic, as is the movie, that many people will think them historically accurate. They are not. There are many inaccuracies, misconceptions, and misunderstandings. I lumped some of these into a single category and just called them "myths." Permit me to point out some of these, but first a little background.

Most of the Civil War, almost all of it, was fought on Southern soil. The citizens of the Northern states were spared the horrors of war on their front lawns. There were two major exceptions. The first of these was the Battle of Antietam Creek (sometimes called Sharpsburg), and the other was the Battle of Gettysburg. Both of these "invasions" of the North by Lee's Army of Northern Virginia were undertaken to convince the Union to let the South go in peace.

Many people believe, even today, that the Confederacy was simply a group of trouble-making outlaw states. The reality, however, is that there is nothing in the United States Constitution to deny the right of a state, any state, to secede from the Union if it so chooses. That is as true now as it was in 1861. Furthermore, not one of the original thirteen colonies–regardless of its geographical location–would have signed the Constitution and joined the Union if it thought it couldn't get out. I repeat for emphasis, *not one would have done so!* But in April 1861 when eleven Southern states exercised that right, Federal troops "invaded" Virginia to prevent secession, and the battle was joined.

Two years later, we come to the three-day Battle of Gettysburg. This was the pivotal battle of the war between North and South where, ironically, the South came in from the north and the North came in from the south.

Why was a battle fought at Gettysburg, a small farming community of 2400 people, in the first place? Lee hadn't planned to fight at Gettysburg. His primary reasons for invading the North were to draw the Union Army of the Potomac away from Richmond, to re-supply his own Army of Northern Virginia from the rich Pennsylvania farmland, and to draw Meade into a fight on favorable ground. Lee was actually making a thrust towards the city of Harrisburg, situated north of Gettysburg. Lee figured that by threatening the capitol of Pennsylvania, Meade would be forced to fight; Lee would win, and a negotiated peace would follow.

Myth: It is one of Gettysburg's enduring myths that Lee thought there was a shoe factory in the town and sent troops there to obtain shoes for his army. The problem with that story is that there was no shoe factory in Gettysburg. In passing near Gettysburg, a small Confederate patrol entered the town foraging for food and other supplies. The patrol ran into an equally small group of Union Militia (not the regular army) stationed in Gettysburg. Surprised, both groups exchanged shots, hastily disengaged, and withdrew to report the incident.

As luck would have it, a Federal reconnaissance patrol of Union cavalry under General John Buford was nearby looking for Lee. Upon being summoned by the militia troops, Buford galloped to the northwest edge of Gettysburg to reconnoiter. Meanwhile Confederate General Harry Heth sent a brigade of infantry under General John Jay Archer to Gettysburg to assess the patrol's report. Neither was aware of the other's presence. Archer's infantry and Buford's cavalry collided on Wednesday morning, July 1, 1863, and the Battle of Gettysburg began. The two armies had literally stumbled into each other.

Cavalry is neither trained nor equipped to fight infantry. In a stand-up fight with infantry, cavalry would almost certainly come off second best.

Buford, of course, was well aware of this; but when he saw a unit of the Army of Northern Virginia northwest of a small town in Pennsylvania, he knew he had found something big. He understood the tactical situation clearly and reacted quickly. First, he sent a galloper ten miles back down the road to notify General John Reynolds and his 1st Corps that he needed help right away. Second, he prepared to fight a delaying action until Reynolds and his infantry could arrive on the scene. It was imperative that the Confederates be prevented from taking Gettysburg with its network of ten intersecting roads and from occupying the high ground on the eastern outskirts of the town, known as Cemetery Ridge.

John Reynolds was perhaps the best field general in the Union army at the time of this battle. He was a career soldier, and his peers held him in high esteem. His service paralleled that of Robert E. Lee. Like Lee, he had served as Superintendent of West Point. Also like Lee, President Abraham Lincoln had offered him command of the Army of the Potomac. General Reynolds respectfully declined the appointment. He felt that he had neither the patience nor the energy to fight both Lee and the Washington Bureaucracy simultaneously, as his predecessors had been required to do. Ironically, it was Reynolds himself who recommended George Meade for the job. Meade's appointment took effect just a few days before the Battle of Gettysburg.

General Reynolds, accompanied only by his staff, arrived on the field by midmorning and took command from Buford. Elements of his 1st Corps began arriving shortly thereafter. By late morning, around ten-thirty, Reynolds completed the task of placing his troops. With Buford's cavalry protecting his flanks, Reynolds men engaged Archer's brigade. A hot firefight ensued. A few minutes later, Reynolds was struck from the saddle by a minie ball and was killed instantly.

Myth: Who shot General Reynolds? The book is silent on this question. The movie, however, depicts a Confederate sniper with a long telescopic sight attached to his rifle hitting Reynolds with a miracle shot of 800 yards–almost half a mile. While that version cannot be disproved, it almost certainly did not happen that way. Historians have pieced together the eyewitness accounts of people who saw the event and assigned probabilities to the various versions of Reynolds' death. The most likely scenario is that a volley of musketry fired by Archer's troops from a distance of less than 100 yards caused Reynolds' death. In the Civil War, a general officer always carried his flag with him so that he could be easily located on the field when needed. Reynolds and his staff would have been in plain sight, a tempting target for Archer's men. At the time Reynolds was hit, several members of his staff and a horse were also struck.

Myth: The crucial fight at Gettysburg took place on the third day. I don't believe that. I believe Lee lost the battle on the afternoon of the first day. Some historians support this position.

Stonewall Jackson died of wounds received at Chancellorsville in May 1863, two months before Gettysburg. Having lost Jackson, Lee reorganized the Army of Northern Virginia. He took one division from Longstreet's I Corps and assigned it to Jackson's II Corps. He then split the II Corps into two corps, giving one to Ambrose Powell (A.P.) Hill and the other Richard S. (Dick) Ewell. Thus, both Hill and Ewell had been corps commanders less than two months.

General Ewell was a competent soldier. His skills had been well honed under Jackson, and he had performed satisfactorily. It is sometimes axiomatic that a person can perform well, perhaps even brilliantly, at one level but not at a higher level. In the *Peter Principle* this was known as "rising to your level of incompetence."

While Ewell was by no means incompetent, he lacked the drive he had displayed at the division level. This may have been the result of the loss of a leg at the Second Battle of Manassas in late August 1862. Whatever the reason, Ewell's lack of initiative was never manifested so much as on that critical Wednesday afternoon.

While A.P. Hill was busily engaged with Buford's cavalry and Reynolds' infantry, Dick Ewell drove Union troops opposing him back through Gettysburg and onto the heights of Cemetery Hill. Having ceded the high ground to his opponent, Ewell inexplicably stopped his attack. Perhaps he thought that he had already done a good day's work. Nobody really knows, but he was probably just being overly cautious. Ewell would do nothing more that day.

Isaac Trimble, his Aide-de-Camp, pleaded with him to continue. Ewell was non-responsive. "Sir, give me a division and I will take that hill," Trimble said. Ewell said nothing. "Sir, give me a brigade and I will take that hill." Ewell was silent. "Sir, give me a good regiment and I will take that hill," Trimble shouted angrily. This was too much for Ewell. "When I want advice from my subordinates, I'll ask for it," he snapped dismissing Trimble. Two days later, Trimble was transferred to A.P. Hill's Corps and led a division in Pickett's Charge.

I'm convinced that Stonewall Jackson would never have let the Yankees keep the high ground, nor would he have stopped the attack while he had both daylight and momentum. Nevertheless, the attack was halted, the window of opportunity closed, and the Union forces dug in on Cemetery Hill. A lot of fine Confederate infantry would be lost the next day attempting unsuccessfully to do what Ewell might have done more easily on that first day. If Ewell had denied the high ground to Meade's forces on July 1, the Battle of Gettysburg might have ended that day.

General Lee himself must have held this same view. After the war in one of his rare interviews he said, "If I had had Stonewall Jackson with me, as far as man can see, I should have won the Battle of Gettysburg."

The second day of the battle was essentially a series of attempts by Lee to dislodge Meade from Cemetery Ridge. The Wheat Field, the Peach Orchard, the Devil's Den, and Colonel Lawrence Chamberlain's brilliant and determined defense of Little Round Top all occurred on that Thursday afternoon. The day ended with little change in the tactical situation.

We now come to Friday, July 3, 1863. This was "do or die" day for Lee. His army was being bled white, his supplies and ammunition were running low, and he had been on foreign ground too long.

Lee perceived that Meade had strengthened his flanks and weakened the center of his line. History showed that Lee was correct in that assessment. The plan "Marse Robert" devised for the third day was simple and direct. It would be an artillery bombardment followed by an infantry charge straight at the center of Meade's line, then held by Winfield Scott Hancock's II Corps. In other words, "Hey diddle diddle; straight up the middle."

Myth: Pickett's Charge has been called, among other things, "the huge mistake." The noted historian Shelby Foote, author of the comprehensive three volume set titled *The Civil War: A Narrative History*, said that Gettysburg was the price the South paid for having Robert E. Lee for its premier field commander. But was it a mistake? The plan was a good one. It should have worked, and it likely would have worked except for one critical factor. The artillery barrage failed!

Lee ordered his artillery chief, Colonel Porter Alexander, to commence firing at one o'clock that afternoon. He told Alexander to expend all his ammunition except for a few rounds per gun for contingency reserve. This would be an all out, maximum effort, no-holds-barred attempt. Colonel Alexander did just that. For two hours, his 185 guns blazed away at the Union line.

The problem was that his guns were firing too high. This was hardly the result of incompetence, for Alexander was good at his job. Rather it was the result of the tactical situation. Alexander's guns were firing uphill at a line of troops and artillery well dug in along a narrow ridgeline. His aim had to be precise. But almost immediately billows of smoke from the black powder used in those days obscured the entire field. Additionally, as each gun fired, its trail (the long leg on which the gun sat balanced) dug further and further into the ground as the recoil of each shot drove the gun backward. So each shot went successively higher and higher. The Confederate artillery was devastating to Meade's rear, but was mostly ineffective against his defensive line—its primary target. The stage was set for disaster.

It was now three o'clock. Lee's infantry charge would consist of two divisions from A.P. Hill's corps and one division from Longstreet's corps. Here is the Confederate Order of Battle:

—Harry Heth's division (A.P. Hill), now commanded by Johnston Pettigrew after Heth was wounded on July 1, consisted of four brigades.
—Dorsey Pender's division (A.P. Hill), now commanded by Isaac Trimble, after Pender was mortally wounded the previous day, consisted of two brigades.

—George Pickett's division (James Longstreet) consisted of three brigades.

Thus the attacking force had a total of nine brigades consisting of 42 infantry regiments–almost 15,000 battle-hardened veterans in all.

Myth: The name of the action on the afternoon of the third day of the battle has forever been called "Pickett's Charge." This is puzzling because it leaves one with the impression that George Pickett was in command. Not so. His boss, James Longstreet, was actually in command. Why it has been called "Pickett's Charge" has long been a mystery. No one really knows the reason. There are lots of theories, of course, but little definitive proof. Pickett was just one of three division commanders given the task of assaulting the ridge. If anything it should have been called "Longstreet's Charge," although I'm sure "Old Pete" was just as happy it wasn't.

Longstreet didn't want to make the charge at all. He tried several times to talk Lee out of it. Longstreet's troops had manned the fortifications on Marye's Heights at Fredericksburg the preceding December. In that battle, Longstreet saw what the rifled musket could do when handled by well-entrenched troops against unprotected Union infantry. It was devastating and deadly. He knew what the outcome of today's battle would be before it began. It would be Fredericksburg in reverse. Longstreet saw it as clearly as if it had already happened.

Failing to dissuade Lee, Longstreet then tried to pass the command to A. P. Hill. His argument was that Hill had two divisions in the fight, while he had only one. Lee would have none of it. He knew that if it could be done, Longstreet would do it and that was that. When the time came to give the order, Longstreet could not even speak it. He could only look away and nod his assent.

The charge, at great cost, failed. Still, it probably would have worked if the artillery had only done its job. A Confederate infantry brigade under General Louis Armistead actually did breach the Union line, but in insufficient numbers to prevail. Union artillery and musketry that should have been decimated by Alexander's artillery hurt the Confederates cruelly. If Lee had broken through Meade's line in force, he could have turned Meade's flanks from the inside and driven him off the ridge. Had that happened, Meade would have been forced to retreat toward Washington. Such an occurrence would almost certainly have resulted in a negotiated peace.

Myth: Both the book and the movie have Lee apologizing to his men as they stream back from the carnage. "It is all my fault," he reportedly said. Such an occurrence is unlikely. In the first place, Lee had no reason to apologize. His plan was a good one. As explained above, it could have worked. As any soldier or military historian will tell you, no battle plan survives the opening volley. At that point, the individual soldier and chance take over. This is sometimes called "the fog of war." Secondly, general officers usually do not apologize for their failures to their men. It is bad for morale. I'm convinced that Lee made no such apology, at least not then or there. Lee did send Jefferson Davis a letter of resignation following the battle, but Davis refused it.

Myth: We finally come to the widely held belief that George Pickett's division was wiped out at Gettysburg. Pickett himself said so. When ordered by Lee to prepare his division for a possible counter attack by Meade, Pickett is said to have replied, "General Lee, I have no division."

Pickett's division was not destroyed, any more than the other two divisions were. Admittedly, casualties were high. Overall, the casualty rate was on the order of 35 to 40 percent, depending on whose numbers you choose to believe. By today's standards, a casualty rate that high would be unthinkable. Even the marines in World War II on Iwo Jima did not suffer such casualties. Also, high casualty rates were not unusual in the days when men stood out in the open and banged away at each other until one side or the other gave way. Actually, it was closer to the norm.

What were the casualties? Here is a summary:

> —Heth's division: Pettigrew himself was wounded slightly, but was killed ten days later. Of his four brigade commanders, one was killed, and one was wounded and captured. Of his 17 regimental commanders, two were killed, four were wounded, and four were captured. The division lost 874 killed and wounded and 500 captured or missing–a total of 1387.

—Pender's division: Trimble was wounded, lost a leg, and was captured. He survived the war. Of his 10 regimental commanders, three were wounded. The division lost 389 killed and wounded and 261 captured or missing–a total of 654.

—Pickett's division: Pickett himself escaped injury, but two of his three brigade commanders were killed. The third was wounded and captured. Of his 15 regimental commanders, eight were killed and seven wounded. The division lost 1382 killed and wounded and 1499 captured or missing–a total of 2881.

Total Confederate casualties for the afternoon were 4922 representing, assuming an attack force of 15,000, an overall casualty rate of 33 percent. These numbers, though, are hard to pin down. Some historians place the number of casualties somewhat higher and the total number of troops engaged somewhat lower. This would, of course, result in a much higher casualty rate percentage-wise. Some estimates for Pickett's casualties run as high as 60 percent. But such numbers are highly suspect, and few historians lend them credence.

I'm comfortable with the numbers shown above. They were obtained from what I believe to be reliable sources. Regardless of the numbers used, you can hardly conclude that the attacking force was wiped out.

After three days of hard fighting, Lee's losses forced him to leave the field and Pennsylvania. Of a total force of 75,054, Lee had lost 3500 killed, 15,250 wounded, and 5250 captured or missing–a total of 24,000 men. This represents an overall casualty rate of 32 percent, or a third of his army.

By contrast, of a total force of 83,289, Meade's losses were 3155 killed, 14,529 wounded, and 5365 captured or missing–a total of 23,049 men representing an overall casualty rate of 28 percent. So you can see that Meade's losses were about the same as Lee's. Such losses testify to the determined and desperate fight put forth by both armies over those three hot July days in 1863.

There was a missed opportunity here, and it was a big one. The preceding September at Antietam, George McClellan squandered an opportunity to destroy Lee's army. By a monumental stroke of good fortune, one of

McClellan's patrols found a copy of Lee's battle plan for Antietam wrapped around three cigars at an abandoned campsite. Had McClellan been more of a field general and a lot less cautious, he could have crushed Lee then and there.

Just as McClellan had been at Antietam, Meade was too cautious at Gettysburg. Instead of counter attacking, Meade simply watched (some say "escorted") while Lee left Pennsylvania and crossed back over into the relative safety of Virginia.

After Lee left, Meade sent a telegram to Lincoln. It read, "The invader has been driven from our soil." Lincoln was livid. He understood what an opportunity Meade had let slip.

Beginning the day following the battle, it began to rain. By the time Lee arrived at the Potomac River, it was swollen and treacherous. If Meade had been Reynolds or even Hancock, he would have trapped Lee on the north side of the river and the war could have ended right there. Just think of the lives that would have been saved and suffering avoided if either McClellan or Meade had taken advantage of the opportunities handed them.

As it was, the war went on for two more bloody years. Both armies suffered more casualties in the two years following the Battle of Gettysburg than in the two years leading up to it.

What an awful, terrible waste!

978-0-595-37019-1
0-595-37019-5

Printed in the United Kingdom
by Lightning Source UK Ltd.
107356UKS00001B/150